D0418331

A Fictional Guide to Scotland

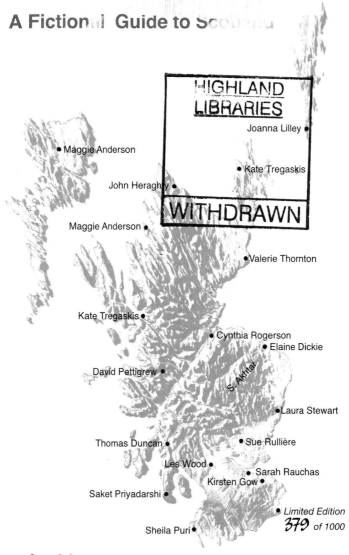

HIGHLAND
LIBRARIES

Joanna Lilley •

• Kate Tregaskis

WITHDRAWN

• Maggie Anderson

John Heraghty •

Maggie Anderson •

•Valerie Thornton

Kate Tregaskis •

• Cynthia Rogerson
• Elaine Dickie

David Pettigrew •

S. Akhtar

•Laura Stewart

Thomas Duncan •

•Sue Rullière

Les Wood •

• Sarah Rauchas
Kirsten Gow •

Saket Priyadarshi •

Sheila Puri •

• *Limited Edition*
379 of 1000

Edited by **OpenInk**
Final contributions chosen by Meaghan Delahunt, Elizabeth Reeder and Suhayl Saadi

Contributions © S. Akhtar, Maggie Anderson, Elaine Dickie, Thomas Duncan, Kirsten Gow, John Heraghty, Joanna Lilley, David Pettigrew, Saket Priyadarshi, Sheila Puri, Sarah Rauchas, Cynthia Rogerson, Sue Rullière, Laura Stewart, Valerie Thornton, Kate Tregaskis, Les Wood, 2003.

Foreword © Elizabeth Reeder, 2003.

First published in the United Kingdom in 2003 by
OpenInk, Glasgow
mail@openink.co.uk
www.openink.co.uk

Cover design and inside title designs by A.R.T. Thomson.

Printed by Cordfall Ltd
Glasgow, G21 2QA

ISBN 0 9545560 0 3

All rights reserved. No part of this book may be reproduced in any form or by any means without the express permission of the publisher, except by a reviewer who may quote brief passages in a review either written or broadcast.

The right of the contributors to be identified as authors of this work has been asserted in accordance with the Copyright, Designs and Patents Act 1988.

The publisher acknowledges support from

 Centre for Lifelong Learning   Scottish **Arts** Council

towards the publication of this volume.

```
┌─────────────────────────┐
│  HIGHLAND               │
│  LIBRARIES              │
│                         │
│                         │
│ ┌───────────┐           │
│ │ WITHDRAWN │           │
│ └───────────┘           │
└─────────────────────────┘
```
HIGHLAND LIBRARIES

WITHDRAWN

Contents

The OpenInk Editorial Board

S. Akhtar
Kirsten Gow
Ashley Lennon
Allan McConnell
David Pettigrew
Colin Poole
Saket Priyadarshi
Elizabeth Reeder
Laura Stewart

Foreword

You hold in your hands our first adventure: our little risk, our commitment; a book that nudges beyond the borders of writing and country and all things that should be infinite – words, minds, possibility. This is not an itinerary of the writing Scotland has produced so far, rather this book takes us into the imagination, to a Scotland that exists in a character, a turn of phrase, in a different world entirely; to a Scotland evoked through the minds of the writers and you, the reader.

As writers, our creativity gathers sustenance in the oddest of places, at the most unpredictable times, and these sparks of passion and strength and shock find voice in the most unprecedented of ways. The places we live, where we come from, the people we meet – all find their way into our writing. As writers we push at boundaries, we take risks and write what most truly compels us; we use observation and pure conjecture to conjure up fictional voices and places.

As citizens, residents, exiles and readers we can do the same things: by imagining other borders, possibilities and futures we can make our countries bigger than their parts, broader than their limitations.

Our little gem, *A Fictional Guide to Scotland*, has been compiled and created by a writer-led non-profit press and is made up of seventeen short stories, one creative non-fiction piece and a poem, all chosen from open, anonymous submissions. This is a leap we took, trusting in the power of the word to guide us: together we are travellers who have a map but no reservations and who want to discover a country as we go along. Are you ready for the trip?

OpenInk's first collection of writing avoids the predictable, sometimes steers clear of even the familiar, and like the boldest of explorers, seeks out what we have not seen before; places and people we have not inhabited. The bravest travellers are those who have no fear of where their imaginations can take them and in *A Fictional Guide to Scotland* a vast inspiring landscape emerges which takes us in, pulls us out of ourselves.

How did we get to this fictitious place? OpenInk started in November 2002 and is made up of nine writers who volunteer as editors and art directors and admin support and publicists and general dogsbodies (sometimes all at once). We wanted to put together a unique, professional collection of writing and support the contributors and the publication through events. Towards this end we brainstormed a name, made an open call for cutting edge writing, applied for funding, received over three hundred submissions in under two months, shortlisted them down to forty-eight pieces, and then, funding confirmed, Meaghan Delahunt, Suhayl Saadi and myself chose the nineteen pieces you will read here.

You will find our long list of thank yous at the back of the book. But here special thanks go to Meaghan Delahunt and Suhayl Saadi, who not only read all the shortlisted pieces, and spent an amazing, electric evening choosing the final stories in my kitchen (Suhayl likened us to three witches, stirring an enormous cauldron of words and silence), but also offered up their time for a few events, all gratis. Suhayl's talent and intelligence are undisputed; Meaghan's openness and wisdom grounded me and inspired me from the moment I first met her, and their participation and generosity are exactly what OpenInk is all about. We are honoured and thrilled that they have been a part of our success.

OpenInk is a communal effort. The board's time and effort, as well as that of friends and supporters, have been donated. Our families have borne the brunt of extra housework and cooking duties while we were off gallivanting at OpenInk fortnightly meetings and, later, when we buried our heads in the resulting 'to dos'. And, as if that wasn't enough, over 40% of the funding for the book and the supporting events came from individual sponsorship volunteered by those same family and friends: a vote of confidence in ourselves, our writing, and our risk taking. The other crucial 60% came from the University of Strathclyde Centre for Lifelong Learning, Glasgow City Council and the Scottish Arts Council and we thank them for their faith in our vision.

OpenInk, run by writers for writers, aims to create a central place of communication, publication and inspiration. We hope that from this place writers will take even bigger risks, will take Scotland further forward, cutting a swathe through the literary world with our words.

Scotland can be a magical place with lochs and steel and concrete, islands and families and friends (old and new), black oil and mountains and seas; with characters on every corner; sheep in every field; and quality silence and space that give you time and leave to process it all. I know that living in Scotland has changed my writing, made it bigger like my view of the world, and that is what we hope you find about this book. Every piece of writing is a path – to a place of rest or restlessness, of revelation or disappointment, private horror or beauty – but I am not going to 'guide' you through this book.

I have found that readers are a smart bunch and I trust you as travellers to find your own paths and make up your own minds.

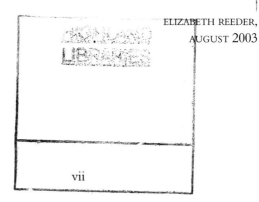

ELIZABETH REEDER,
AUGUST 2003

vii

When Stevie was Married

John Heraghty •

Stevie lived in a small dying town beside the sea. It suited him. He arrived one day, along with a squad of men, to work on a job rewiring the local primary school. One weekend, when the rest of the men were going back home to their families in the city, he decided to stay on. He booked himself into a local Bed and Breakfast and spent the next couple of days exploring the town. He had lived all his life in the city among people, noise and smoke, and liked the idea of living somewhere quiet and anonymous. Somewhere he had no history in. After the job was finished the rest of the squad moved on to another school in another town. Stevie stayed.

He bought a small van and started to work for himself. There was always someone needing electrical work done. Farmers building new sheds, shopkeepers renovating their premises and in the small towns nearby there were new houses and schemes being built. Stevie would turn up in his van and be hired immediately. He was a good electrician and there was always a shortage of good men.

Stevie soon found a rhythm to his life in the town. A rhythm that suited him. He found a flat to live in and a pub to drink in. That was all he needed. The flat was a one room and kitchen that looked onto the sea. The pub was called The Eagle and had a satellite dish outside. After work each day he would go in for a couple of pints of lager and then go home and make his dinner. After dinner he would read the paper, watch the news and then wash some of his work clothes. At ten o'clock he would head back to the pub for the final hour.

After a short time he became a local. Watched the football when it was on satellite television. Was on first name terms with the bar staff. Got on nodding terms with the other regulars who had their own corner beside the door. After a few months he got into conversations with the other locals about work and football. Soon Stevie had his own seat at the bar.

One night, just before closing, Stevie decided that he was married. The men had got into a conversation about food and what kind of lunch their wives made for them to take to work each day. Stevie was listening in as he sipped his lager. One of the men asked him what kind of lunch his wife sent him out with in the morning. He thought for a moment and then said:

— It's brilliant.

And from that moment on, Stevie was married.

Why not? Why not invent a new life, he thought as he walked home from the pub that night. He was still a stranger in the town, no one knew anything about him. He could be anyone he wanted to be. He liked the idea of making up a new life. Inventing himself. He could be an ex-boxer. Played in a band. Served in the army; couldn't talk about it, hush hush. Was out on licence. Maybe he had to get out of the city because he was caught up in low-level criminal activity involving loose tobacco. Anything was possible. On his way home from the pub, Stevie realised the opportunity he had to really start a new life for himself.

He decided that being married was part of this new life. Stevie had never been married and when he thought of the future he thought of himself as being alone. Now he could have any wife he wanted. Stevie decided that his wife would be a great cook and the next time the conversation came up at the bar he gave the rest of the drinkers an idea of the quality and variety of the meals she prepared for him. In the morning after a cooked breakfast she would send him off to work with a lunch box packed full of sandwiches, crisps, biscuits and a piece of fruit too, ensuring he had a balanced diet. When he came home from work there would be a bowl of home-made soup waiting for him and then a main meal made with chicken or steak. His wife enjoyed cooking and trying out new dishes. She would visit local farms outside the town for fresh produce: hen eggs, duck eggs, potatoes, onions and chickens. As they listened to Stevie talk, the other men at the bar were envious of the attention his wife paid him. They would send out for take-away meals most nights and if their wives made something it was either undercooked or burnt.

Stevie was enjoying his new married life until his wife turned up. One evening he went into the fruit shop at the end of his road to pick up some potatoes and turnips when the fruit man told him that his wife had been in earlier that day and had collected his messages. He walked out of the shop empty handed and stood and thought for a moment. No, it must be someone else. The fruit man was confusing him with someone else. The next evening he went into the pub as usual after work. He ordered his pint of lager and as Liz the barmaid was putting his drink in front of him, she told him his wife was just off the phone, asking if he could bring a bottle of wine home for dinner. He looked at the men at the bottom of the bar who winked and said:

— Something special the night again Stevie, eh?

— Aye. Aye.

He finished his drink quickly and went home. He put his key carefully in the lock and opened the door. He didn't know what to expect. When he went in, the flat was the same as he had left it that morning. What was going on? In the following week there were no phone calls or sightings in the fruit shop and Stevie forgot about it.

Then one evening he opened the door and there she was. His wife. Sitting on the couch watching early evening TV.

— Hi darling, she said, dinner won't be too long. What kind of day did you have? Good day? Bad day? Sit down here. I'll get you a drink and you can tell me all about it.

Stevie stood in the centre of the room and his wife went into the kitchen. A few moments later she returned with a can of lager and a glass. She sat on the couch and poured the drink. When she had finished pouring she looked up at Stevie and handed him the glass.

5

Stevie was still standing in the centre of the room. She smiled at him.

— Quiet tonight darling. You tired? You must have had a hard day. Don't worry, I've got your favourite for dinner tonight.

He had ham broth and a chicken curry and it was beautiful. She was as good a cook as he said she was. After dinner he sat down on the couch. His wife came to join him and picked up the remote control and switched the TV on. She knew all the programmes he watched, first the soap, then the gardening and then the news. She switched to the right channel just as they were about to start, making sure they didn't miss anything.

Stevie went out to the pub as usual that night. He needed time to think. Sitting at the bar he wondered how this had come about. Maybe the guys in the pub found out he wasn't really married and were trying to wind him up. He had talked too much about her and annoyed them; now they were getting their own back. The other regulars were at their usual seats and nodded to him and asked how the wife was.

— Fine, he said and studied their faces carefully, but there were no smiles or smirks. No one was giving the game away.

When he went back home that night his wife was in bed sleeping. She had arranged a fresh pair of pyjamas and left them on his side of the bed. The room was warm and smelled fresh and natural. Getting into bed, he couldn't remember the last time he had slept with a woman. When he pulled the covers up he could feel the warmth coming from his wife and it felt nice after the cold walk home. She turned over in her sleep and cuddled up close to him. The sensation was strange, feeling someone warm beside him in the bed.

When he woke up the next morning the bed was empty. He wondered, had it been a dream? Stevie pulled on his work clothes and went to make his breakfast. When he opened the bedroom door he was met with the smell of bacon frying. In the kitchen, the table was set for two. His wife squeezed by him and put a plate of toast down on the table.

— Morning darling, she said and kissed him on the cheek.

— Sorry I wasn't awake last night. I was tired out. You look fresh this morning. Did you have a good snooze?

— Yeah. Yeah I did.

— Good. Good. Here we are.

She went over to the cooker and came back with two plates that she put on the table. Two plates of a fully cooked breakfast. Bacon. Sausage. Egg. Tomato. Fried Bread. Black Pudding. 'The Works' it was called. He realised he was hungry and sat down and tucked in. The breakfast was delicious and when he had finished she gave him a lunch box on his way out the door. Outside he looked in the box. It was packed with his favourites – a cheese and pickle sandwich, a couple of packets of crisps, a Penguin bar and a banana.

When he got home that evening the living room had been changed around. The sofa had been moved from in front of the window and now sat against the wall. Beside the window there was a small table he had never seen before. On the table there was a vase with fresh purple-coloured flowers. On the walls of the room there were photos hanging in frames. He moved nearer and saw that the photos were of him. Him and his wife. Their wedding day. On their honeymoon. Visiting London: a picture of them both standing outside Buckingham Palace. The two of them standing beside Mickey Mouse in Florida. A picture of them enjoying a romantic candlelit dinner. Stevie looked closely at the pictures. It was definitely him.

— Hope you like the room. Thought we could do with a bit of a change.

— Yeah, it's nice, he said, looking at his wife.

He had a lovely dinner again that night and the next night and the night after that. Soon he had been married a week and then a month. After two months Stevie started to get used to the new arrangement.

Stevie's wife's name was Jackie and she was lovely; a few years younger than him, she had dark brown hair and brown eyes. She was tall and dressed very smartly even in the house. He could tell that she looked after herself. Stevie had done well. He could see that.

He stopped going to the pub straight from work and would go home instead. He would talk to Jackie and tell her what kind of day he'd had, where he was working, who he was working with. And she would tell him about what she had watched on the telly, who she met when she was out shopping. He started to look forward to seeing her and as he drove home in his van he would think of what he would tell her about his day.

Instead of going to the pub he started to go for long walks with Jackie along the sea front. She persuaded him to buy a small dog that they called Dusty. The three of them would be out every evening walking beside the kiosks and amusement arcades. Stevie had a stick and would throw it along the pebbly beach. Dusty would chase after the stick and bring it back to him and drop it at his feet. They bought ice creams and sat and watched the sun go down before they made their way home. At weekends they would go for long drives in Stevie's van and stop somewhere and climb a hill for a few hours. On their way home they would go into a pub and have lunch together. Dusty would sit beside them on the floor, drinking water from a bowl they carried in the van. Stevie would drink a bottle of lager and his wife would drink a dry white wine. This would be the only time of the week that Stevie would be in a pub.

Stevie started to take better care of himself. After work he would have a shower and change into fresh clothes. He had his hair cut short and shaved every day. They went shopping and Jackie helped him pick some new clothes. He bought a smart pair of jeans, a checked shirt, new shoes, a sweater and a jacket. He looked fine, he thought to himself as he pulled his stomach in. The home-made cooking had put an extra inch around his waist.

He started making an effort. Stevie hadn't made an effort in a long time. He would buy his wife small gifts, something he would see in a shop when he was on his break. A scented candle. A key ring. A book of ghost stories. He liked buying his wife things and liked to see the look on her face when he placed some carefully wrapped present on the table or sat it beside the cooker while she was stirring a sauce. She said he had good taste and he enjoyed being a man with good taste.

Stevie started thinking about Jackie while he was at work. He would phone her to ask how she was. And he would worry if she didn't answer the phone. When he did make contact she would tell him she had been out shopping or taken the dog for a walk and not to be silly, she was all right. He had been so used to being on his own he forgot what it was like living with another person. There were two of everything in the flat. Two sets of clothes. Two sets of bedcovers. Two sets of dishes. The place seemed full up.

He liked getting to know his wife and noticing her odd habits, like the way she brushed her teeth and tried to talk to him at the same time when they were going to bed at night. She always ended up dribbling some of the white toothpaste on her chin. He would take a towel and gently wipe the toothpaste away and give her chin a soft kiss. She would smile at him and give him a hug. Stevie was thrilled by these small, delicate moments of intimacy.

Stevie couldn't remember a time that he wasn't married. He forgot about his single life, going to the pub on his own, cooking for himself, being silent. He enjoyed being with someone, thinking about them, worrying about them, looking after them. He thought about when he was growing up and the hopes he had and how he wanted to meet someone and settle down, and now, after all these years, it was happening.

One day Stevie came home from work and his wife was gone. It was a Friday evening and Stevie was looking forward to the weekend and what they would do together. He had bought a box of chocolates for Jackie and had driven home fast. He ran up the stairs of the close two at a time, smiling to himself. But when he opened the door she wasn't there. The flat was back to the way it had been when he first moved in. The sofa was against the window blocking out the light. The walls were bare; the photos gone. Her clothes were gone. Her toothbrush was gone. The food cupboards were empty and the exotic spices all gone. Dusty, Dusty's basket and bowls were all gone. He sat down on the couch and looked at the box of chocolates he was holding. He had been looking forward to watching her taking the wrapper off and opening the box, to seeing her smile when she spotted her favourite – the Russian Caramel.

Stevie went out that evening and walked along the front alone. When he came back and opened the door to the flat he was hoping that she would be there. But the flat was empty, silent. He went out every evening and walked along by the sea and thought of the times they had together, the things she said to him, the clothes she wore. As he walked, he passed people who would smile sympathetically. Stevie missed his wife.

Stevie started going into the fruit shop again and bought a bag of potatoes every Friday. He had no lunch box now and wherever he was working he would look for a café or a van that served all-day breakfasts. He stopped shaving every day, only doing it once or twice a week, and he put his good clothes away in the wardrobe.

One evening after work Stevie went into The Eagle and ordered a pint. The usual crowd were at their corner of the bar. He nodded over at them. His seat was still there. Liz came and put a pint of lager in front of him.

— That's from the boys, Stevie. Sorry to hear about the wife.

— No luck big man, one of the regulars said and the rest nodded their heads in agreement.

Stevie nodded back and sipped his pint of lager.

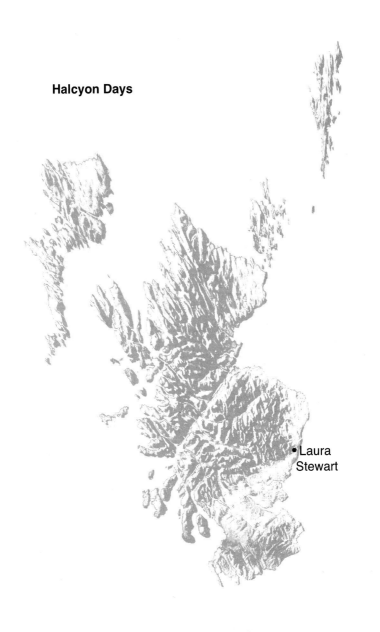

Halcyon Days

Laura
Stewart

The Gods gave Ava Kingfisher lips like cherry sweets: plump, sticky and unreal red. They formed a perfect bow drawn taut over strong white teeth, which women feared would fire off suggestive arrows aimed at their husbands' hearts.

The Gods carved Miss Kingfisher's exquisitely shaped shoulders from the finest Carrara marble and made them strong enough to carry the burden of a single mother's load.

They bestowed on her two almond-shaped emeralds for eyes. And they gave her a storyteller's voice: rich and low, as beguiling as smoke caught behind glass, ready to tell of handsome princes with eyes the colour of lapis lazuli, their silver breastplates protecting hearts and their swords carving out their honour.

As girl became woman, this abundance of beauty became balanced with a kindness and trust, leaving her vulnerable to emotional bruising. Lovers melted away from her as they realised they would never tame the flights of fancy they saw in her eyes. One night, as she flicked through a magazine whilst waiting for a man whose promises had long turned to dust, Ava Kingfisher saw an advert for a beauty contest on Fiji. She didn't care for the prize money or trinkets on offer, nor did she covet the honour of winning. Within the photograph of the island she saw adventure and possibilities; she saw white sand which would feel like silk as it yielded beneath her bare feet; she saw lush banana leaves framing an eternal blue sky; she saw escape from the drab grey her world had become. With no other thought to her life in Scotland, Miss Kingfisher flew to the sanctuary of the 1969 World Beauty Pageant.

The organisers, setting the procedure on a remote Fijian island, had remained aesthetically blinkered, choosing not to heed the warnings of the unpredictable weather. One square mile of the world's most beautiful roses had, inevitably, to suffer a thorn. It arrived in the form of a hurricane; a bellyache from Zeus himself, gatecrashing the post-ceremony party, wiping away all the camera equipment along with Miss Italy, Miss Iceland and herself, Ava Kingfisher.

Clutching her runner-up's tiara with one hand and a dinghy with the other, Miss Kingfisher floated on the South Pacific Ocean through the night, scared to move for fear of tipping the boat. High above, Castor and Pollux spent the night shielding the dinghy from the attention-seeking wind and rain, and next morning, when the sun rose, it was to peaceful skies with all hostility forgotten.

Miss Kingfisher bobbed against the waves, growing feverish with the white heat of the sun burning through her eyelids as he boldly watched from above. And as a hot fuchsia and orange sunset ripped into the sky on the second night, a humble fishing boat, thrown slightly off by a storm-damaged rudder, picked her up and hauled her on board, where she lay amongst the day's catch. The younger crew watched in awe until the wiser captain took charge, pouring water through her dried lips and smoothing cocoa butter onto her burning skin.

On reaching dry land, the fishermen carried her to a little yellow hut on the beach where a kind woman smiled down at her, showing ten golden teeth and a wad of chewing tobacco. She administered an infusion of coconut oil and sugar cane and when Miss Kingfisher threw it all back up again the woman laughed loud and long, holding her quivering belly. This woman called herself Aphrodite and she knew about matters of the heart and the consequences.

Aphrodite laughed and sang while preparing a dinner full of love and a pound of the island's finest ginger to calm the sickness and help the unborn baby grow strong with a warm heart. And with a smile as wide as the heavens, the gold-toothed woman renamed the visitor Little Bird.

A sequinned evening gown proved impractical for everyday island dwelling and Aphrodite gave Little Bird fabric of the deepest blues and greens fashioned into a dress to accommodate the bump, which swelled with sunshine, good food and well wishes.

Days turned to weeks and Little Bird put off leaving, her unbalanced hormones seeking reasons to stay on the island she considered home. One day Poseidon would anger the waves into rabid froth, with no boat able to sail, the next Aeolus would release the winds and everyone would take shelter in their homes and swap stories of their beautiful island. Then one day Little Bird became too pregnant to fly and instead settled onto a houseboat nestled in a sheltered cove.

Each night she relived her nightmare on the dinghy: cast adrift and helpless, feeling the burden of fear weighing her down, pulling her under the water, where the seaweed formed into the face of the father of her unborn child. She'd kiss each line of his face, feel his water-slicked skin against her own flesh, memorising the exact colour of his eyes she was determined never to forget. But on waking, terror caught in her throat and he disappeared from her, a film of gauze separating them, blurring colour and shapes. And she couldn't remember anything from that one frantic night, only that she'd loved him for a little while, until it was obvious he had no intention of returning.

Cradling her belly, she would sing softly under her breath, her sweet words carrying across the water, guiding sailors safely ashore.

She delivered her child beside the sea. Sofia had an abundance of jet-black hair and large limpid eyes and Little Bird decided that with no money and no real home, she would have to return to her village in Scotland, her life and being Miss Kingfisher.

She spent her last night on the island sitting by a beach fire with Aphrodite, who pressed a red rose and a whale tooth into the palm of her hand and told her to always follow her dreams, for one day they would come true.

Returning home was not easy. The small village contained equally small minds and Miss Kingfisher did not fit into their grey caged world. As years passed, she refused to clip her wings and held onto her daughter as dearly as she held the conviction that Aphrodite spoke the truth.

Whilst out walking, Miss Kingfisher would smoke the multi-coloured Russian cigarettes with the silver tip and tell stories to the men and children who would listen, transfixed, as her elegant arms arced wide. She talked animatedly of the past, cigarette holder wafting high smoke circles in the air, a signal caught on the breeze, beckoning others in, bewitching them with lavish tales. When she had been a model, when she was slimmer, she would laugh, patting her concave stomach.

Summers were the best and like a bunch of Victorian ragamuffins, the village children, led by Sofia, would wander from house to garden to burn, looking for muddy adventures, living halcyon days of rain-free afternoons, a docken leaf beside every stinging nettle and unsupervised play.

No matter what mischief they sought, the children would always materialise at Miss Kingfisher's house at lunchtime, drawn by homely aromas. Miss Kingfisher, whilst proving the bread, proved her aptitude to home-making by home-baking. Once fed, the boys would run off to sit in the wild overgrown grass that neighbours called a disgrace, but children simply thought magical. The girls, however, would hover by the kitchen in case Miss Kingfisher felt like talking.

One day a bee stung Sofia. Hysterical at the pain and the swelling of her arm, she cried as her friends looked from the dying bee rolling on the ground to the end of the sting, protruding from the reddening flesh like an exclamation mark. Silently following her into the house, they watched Miss Kingfisher empty her make-up bag in search of tweezers. Little pots of cream and expensive lipsticks rolled along the counter as Sofia's cries changed to subdued whimpers. The girls clustered around, rifling through the luxurious jars and potions, far removed from their own mothers' sparse collection of greasy foundations and flat-blue eyeshadows. Curious fingers dipped into pearlescent turquoises and created paths of uncharted territory across eyes and cheeks.

A woman's beauty can be her weapon, Miss Kingfisher told them, twisting open a sparkling magenta lipstick and dabbing shimmer onto waiting lips. Then she told them the story of Helen, whose own lips were as soft as a breeze on a petal and whose cheeks had the contours of the finest sand dunes. And she told them of the Trojan War, the consequence of such beauty. Then she sent the children home, waiting for the silent disapproval, the angle of the head, just so, as mothers reacted to the painted faces and colourful notions.

Sitting back and lighting a cigarette, Miss Kingfisher let the smoke curl around her head, hazing the present and opening the gates to her past. She looked to a grainy photograph nestled within an untarnished brass frame: three smiling woman laughed into the camera, hands shielding eyes from the sun, obscuring recognition, sashes resting on bikini-clad jutting hips. With no other surviving footage, it was all that remained of the 1969 World Beauty Pageant. Looking past the figures, the roof of the beach hut was barely visible and she could hear Aphrodite laughing as she gutted a fish to cook on the fire. The familiar ache of longing was joined by a new sensation. In the centre of her rib cage, at the core of her being, she felt a deep desire for excitement. She longed for the sweet smell of sandalwood and it travelled on the sigh of her hope towards the heavens. Zeus, waking from ambrosia sleep, became enrobed by the resinous aroma and remembered the beautiful woman he had lovingly created. Morpheus showered her with poppies and she fell into a sleep as deep as death. She dreamt of a man with the wisdom of the ocean in his eyes. He told her his name was Speranza and whispered promises of rugged adventure.

The next morning she woke to find him waiting patiently by her front gate. He reached out a muscular arm, sun-kissed to conker brown, and pulled Ava Kingfisher and Sofia onto his indigo caravan, pulled by his horse named Fate.

As they ambled slowly from the village, an audible sigh of relief could be heard from wives as they loosened their hands from their portly husbands' arms. And the men knew they would never again look longingly at the elegant line of calf turning to ankle as Miss Kingfisher walked by.

Cut-Price Laundry on Mocha Street

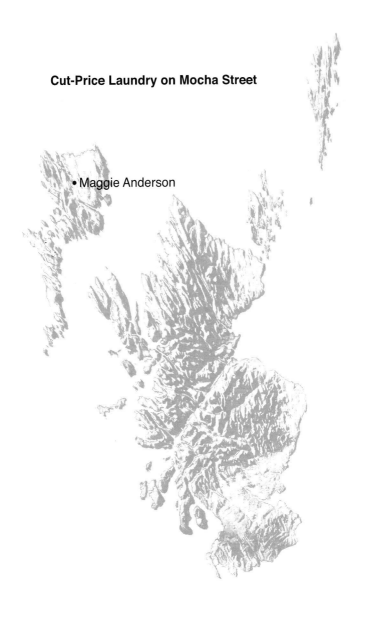

• Maggie Anderson

DAUGHTER

Ayesha was wife to the prophet Muhammad, *blessings on his name*. She could read and write though he could not. I have her name and I'm learning as she did. Soon I will know what the newspapers say. Someday, *if it is God's will*, I will write for them.

I'm sixteen. I live to wash and iron clothes all day. I run up and down the hot broken stairs to the wires strung across the blazing roof. I pin out wet shirts to look like hanged men. I have to watch out for sandstorms. The last time the shemal blew I took a whole day to clean the sand from the roof and stairs. Rain isn't often a problem. When that blessing comes people are too busy, dancing in puddles, to complain if their washing isn't ready. I haven't been to school but I can pen numbers on garments, and count the money they bring. My father takes it all.

My brother is twenty-two. He has been to a technical college, and wants to be an oil worker in the Gulf. He is my secret teacher. I will learn to write to him. When he sends us money, *God willing*, my father plans to close the washing business. I will not be kept at home if my father doesn't need my labour. I pray these things will happen before I am too old to be married to a young man. I know from the cinema, and from my brother, that some young men these days do not want to have children. I dream of such a man. At the cinema there is often music. I watch the hands of the musicians stroking their lutes and drumskins, and I think of these long brown hands moving over my skin. The insides of my belly begin to move and I feel faint, warm, happy. Then I remember the pain. I have no friend that I can ask about the strange feelings, no one to talk to about the agony of when I was made a pure woman.

If I have to stay here much longer I will be given to an old man who has been married before. My sister Amina was married five years ago to a widower with six children at home. Now she has two sons of her own. At twenty-one, cooking and cleaning for ten, she looks old like my mother. She says that she will die of the pain if she has to have another child. How can I ask her about my feelings? We are permitted to go to the cinema sometimes, but I get beaten if my father thinks I have been helping at her house.

I laughed at Amina when she told me that European women wear small trousers under their skirts. They have to pull them down every time they go to the latrine. How do they manage? They must get in a mess. I know they wear lots of attar. I can smell its sweetness if one of them is standing near me at the market. *God the provider* must give many roses to Europe. My sister says that these women don't have to be cut. Are they a different shape? My father says that all white women are whores, but I am sure he is wrong. My brother says they speak kindly, and teach him well in the college. He likes their flower perfume.

I make my teeth shine with a toothstick from the vegetable market. I keep mine under the pillow of my bed to chew every night and morning. My mother and Amina keep theirs with a house-key in their bras. I refuse to wear such a garment. Goats in the street have their udders tied up in cloth. I want to feel my breasts moving under my blouse. What can my mother do about it?

I like my hair. It is waist long and wavy. I am glad not to have tight curls. Sometimes, when I clean it with a lump of charcoal and rub it with oil, I can see red and gold lights in the black. Although I have a big bottom, like my mother, my legs are slim and straight, my waist narrow. I hate my rough hands and broken nails, but my little brother finds them gentle enough. He laughs when I stroke and tickle him. My mother buys cactus juice to soothe our hands. She put it on her nipples to stop the baby feeding. He spat and yelled, but learned to eat porridge from her finger.

Sometimes I think I'd rather wash other people's clothes all my life than have babies. I wake in the night. There are hands holding me down and raging cutting pain. I hear women's voices shrill, '*Thanks be to God*'. How can I be a pure whole woman when a dirty knife defiled so much of my body? If I had to be cut, why did they pay an old women to do it on a filthy rock in a stinking tent? Why did my own mother help them? The tooth she broke with her stick still cuts my tongue.

I used to like going to market with my mother until one day we went early. She bought expensive fruit – mangoes and guavas – instead of ordinary bananas. There were dates too, smoked cheese which I love, and dark honey. At home she packed this in a basket and we got dressed in our best clothes. We were going to visit friends I had never heard of in a village in the desert. When an old taxi came for us we left my father and brother looking after the washing. We were on holiday.

The road was along the beach, at low tide. The car splashed through pools of water and bumped over the sand. How we laughed. We saw eagles fishing and dolphins jumping out of the water. Mother said that they were chasing fish. There were men washing their camels in the sea. The animals sat in the shallows, chewing, as buckets of water were poured over them. We saw fishermen pulling in nets of sardines. Mother wanted to buy some, but the driver said there was no time to stop. He said the tide would come in before we reached the road to our village. I think he didn't want smelly fish in his car. He played music on the radio and my mother and I clapped each other's rough hands in time.

At the end of the beach a track took us inland to a beautiful garden. Here we had our picnic under neem trees, double the size of the straggly one in our backyard. Little yellow birds were weaving nests of straw that looked like baskets hanging from the branches. Green parrots screamed go-away warnings at me. I laughed. The gardener was growing sesame and tomatoes. There was henna too. He gave me a rose but the only smell was the guava juice on my hands. He showed me the plants in the hedge. The spines were as long as my thumb and sharp as needles. We drank cold water from a well and squatted giggling among the bushes. I had never been so happy in my life.

After the garden the road was over rocky desert. The car was hot. Dust stuck to our sweaty skin. The special honey – it was all for me – had made me sleepy. My head lay in my mother's lap and she stroked my hair.

There was a noisy welcome when we reached the village. Women were dancing, hand-clapping, singing. We were led to a black tent where I was made to sit on a flat stone. I was still very drowsy so my mother sat behind me. I lay back against her, listening lazily to the drumming and singing, as the women came in. I watched their silver chains and bracelets swaying to the music. The dust rose from the sandy floor, stirred by their jingling stamping feet.

I came to my senses when an old woman in black bustled in calling out our names with welcome and blessings. She danced round the rock honouring us, her special guests, with a shrill song, *thanks be to God*. She stopped in front of me, and I saw that she held an old rusty razor. My father shaves with a sharp shiny one. She spat on it and wiped it on her skirt. When our eyes met I understood that her foul knife was to be used on me.

I should not have screamed. That let my mother force a stick between my teeth and tie my jaws together over it. My skirt was pressed up round my face to blind me. I couldn't breathe. There were hands everywhere. I felt rings and bracelets pressing hard into my head, arms, body, and pulling my legs apart. How many shrieking women held me down?

The slicing searing agony, as parts of me were torn off and thrown on the bloody sand, went on and on for months in my brain and body, through endless fevers as I healed. The needle thorns, used to skewer my cut flesh together, dried and were pulled out. I remembered the hedge at the picnic garden and told myself to die. When my mother took me walking to market for the first time, nearly a year later, I fainted on the road. She said it was the heat, but I smelled guava fruit from two streets away. She nursed my recovery, but I will never speak to her. She should remember that she closed my mouth herself. The she-devil in the tent sang as she took my father's money to make me a pure whole woman. My mother said, *God is merciful.*

Last year, when the clean cooking knife cut into my hand in the kitchen, my parents rushed me to hospital. The gentle doctor gave me a needle that took away the pain, and pills to keep away the yellow rot that I knew to fear. He made tiny stitches that melted away. My finger, *praise be to God*, is as good as new. I was able to work again very soon. The rest of my body is damaged for always. I will never be the mother of a girl like me.

In the corner of our yard there is a stinking hole we have to pee in. When I was small I ran in and out quickly. Now it takes so long – trickle, burn, drip, burn. I feel ill every morning and evening. I dread to go. How long would it take for a husband to stab his seed into me, and for his baby to tear its way out? I wonder about my sister with her husband, but we talk of other things. I want to be a working woman, not a mother.

The only music I hear is from the café in the street. The owner is my father's friend. His wife is dead and he lives with his three sons. They look after customers who come to eat, drink coffee, smoke and play trictrac. I have never been there, but all day I hear the voices of men from the café. I smell fragrant rice cooking and cumined meat on hot coals. I hope they smell my soap and steam.

When I wash their clothes I take special care of a green shirt with wide, gold-embroidered sleeves. The cloth is rubbed on the front. I think it is where the youngest son holds his lute. I have never seen, but can imagine, his hands on the strings. He sings and plays for the customers. Sometimes his friends join him with drums and flutes. The men dance. I go to the roof to listen. *God forgive me*, I loosen my hair and blouse to dance. I wish the lute player could see me. I make my bangles jingle in time to the music. I want to have anklets of bells and tiny brass cymbals for my fingers. I have seen the gypsy girls dancing in the street. I want to dance with them. My sister says that they are whores. She blesses the nights she sleeps alone in peace, *thanks be to God* for what they do.

My bangles are glass. They dance in the soapy water and sparkle in the sun. Today I have three on one arm and one on the other. When my father next goes to Friday prayers I will put all four on one arm. That counts four weeks, and I'll be waiting for my time of blood and pain to come. I know I will ache when the inside of my body moves by itself, and my back wants to break. My mother will rub it with ice in a cloth, or a hot smooth stone. She'll perhaps give me a poppy head to suck, as she would to a crying baby. Then I will feel better, *thanks be to God*. I will not thank her. It is her duty.

I have to sit on my bed for two days, happy with my book, but unclean, forbidden to touch even the butcher's bloodstained shirts. The old woman in the black tent said I would be pure. Why is the blood of a sheep cleaner than mine?

MOTHER

I am Fatima, wife for twenty-three years to Ali the laundry man. He is a good husband and, *thanks be to God*, we have two fine strong sons. There are also two daughters.

My son Abdul has an air ticket to the Gulf where he will look for a job in an oil refinery. We worked for years to gather the money for his schoolbooks and college fees. I cannot read the gold writing on his diploma, but I kissed the red wax seal. *God forgive my pride*. I have the photograph of my son on the wall beside my bed. I am glad that he will go away for he is to send us money. We will be able to stop washing clothes and, *God willing*, join a café business. He has been teaching his second sister Ayesha to read and write. He says that she is more clever than some of the boys in college. How can this be true?

My next born was a girl, Amina. I had a lot of worry with her. Her skin tore open and bled into the soapy water. She couldn't hold the hot irons. She had an illness when she was nine, and one leg never worked well after it. So she was useless to us for washing the clothes, or limping up to the roof with them. Sometimes she made a little money helping our neighbours with their children.

When we heard of a widow man needing a mother for his six boys, we were able to marry her off. Now, *thanks to the Almighty*, she has two sons. Of course she is tired but her husband is old. She tells me that he does not trouble her often. With ten in the house she is glad of my visits when I can leave her sister working here. Her husband's sons will marry soon and new daughters-in-law will help her. She will always have a home, *thanks be to God*, even if her husband dies. Amina is happy with this. She talks no nonsense about school and reading. Why should she care about newspapers with sons to look after her?

Ayesha was a beautiful happy child. She still has the golden skin that turned heads in the market when she was a girl. I was proud to have her with me. My husband's friends made many offers for her then. The purple insect bite on her cheek is a pity, but it does show up the paleness of her smooth skin, and it matches her lips. They remind me of dark grapes. I know she takes my coconut oil for her hair. I am not angry about this. I get cactus juice to soothe our soapy hands. We have to be careful not to use this at food times. It has a horrible taste.

Ayesha has not spoken to me for four years. She does her duty and works very hard. She does everything she is told: washes, cleans, cooks, sews, goes to the market. She will not talk to me. Her own mother is a stranger to her. I suppose it happened after I took her to the women in the desert, to be cut. She hardly cried then – just one great scream. It wakes me still at night. She wept no tears then or later, but she took a long, hard time to heal. She didn't cry last year when she cut her hand. I am sure she did that on purpose to get away from soapy water. We had to spend a lot of money at the hospital. We needed her back at work but, *God is generous*, and her hand was better in two days.

I can understand her hatred. I never had anything more to do with the aunt who took me to the desert tent, because my mother was in childbirth. Auntie kept me till I healed. She sent me home when my mother died. My father needed me to take care of my baby brother. He has grown and loves someone else now. Babies are the only people who really love you. At first they need you. Then they don't. But *God is merciful and compassionate* and another child will bring more love.

Ayesha loves my little son. She tells stories, sings and dances for him. He follows her everywhere, except the roof. Sometimes I think he likes her more than me, his mother. When she has her monthly pain she accepts the help I give her, but utters no thanks. She sits on her bed, daring me with her eyes to take away the book that her brother Abdul has given her. I have had her father beat her for running away to Amina, and for this reading nonsense. She doesn't seem to care. How will we get her a good marriage? We certainly cannot afford to keep her when my husband stops the washing business.

I told Amina to explain to her that being a woman is meant to be hard. The pain of having children makes you love them more. It is her duty to marry the man we arrange for her. She told Amina that she wants to have a husband that she loves. He must be in love with her. She wants to choose a man. *God forgive me* for allowing her to learn this nonsense at the cinema. She has told Amina that she does not want to have any children. The pain is great and we all fear it.

It is God's will.

Baby Ahmed is two. For his education and future we will sell our list of washing customers to that family in Sokkar Street who are going to buy machines. We plan to join with the café business next door. My husband's friend, the owner, can afford to repair our crumbling stair and roof. Customers will enjoy looking down on the crowded noisy pavement. We can easily make the roof beautiful with cushions and a few plants in pots. Ayesha and I will cook and clean. The men will look after the customers. Of course Ayesha will be married to one of the sons or, better, to the father. When she is settled, with a husband and a home for the rest of her life, she will, I am sure, talk to me again. We will be partners in the business.

Ayesha chatters to her sister Amina about the youngest son of our neighbour. He plays his lute in the café in the evenings. Sometimes at the weekends I hear loud music when his friends come with drums and flutes. The men dance round them. This music has bewitched her. When she hears them practice in the daytime, I can hardly get any work out of her. I caught her dancing, a green shirt in her hands, hair flying loose. I was afraid of the look in her eyes. I couldn't tell her father to punish her

She must stop thinking about the handsome lute player. He has refused to marry her, or any other girl. He's going off to the city to make music with the drummer boy in the band. *If it is God's will* he will become rich and famous. He isn't interested in being a good husband or father. My husband must speak to our daughter about this.

No, she must marry the father. As the wife of this hard-working man she will have authority over the wives of his sons. I, Fatima, her mother, wife of the business partner, will rule them all. Ayesha will be made to see that this is the best solution. *Everything is in the hands of God.*

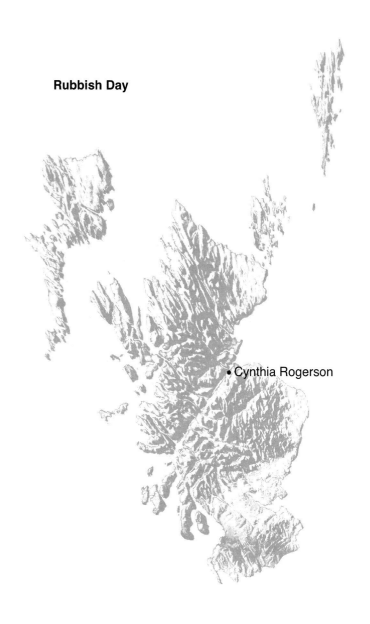

Rubbish Day

• Cynthia Rogerson

J ust after I lose my job, I lose my kid. It's like Jack died without me noticing, and I forgot to have a proper funeral so I can't even grieve properly. I have to act like it's not surreal and sad that he's been replaced by a sweaty dour stranger. Plus it seems I have become equally repulsive to him. An embarrassment who drives the wrong car, wears the wrong clothes. Suddenly, I can't even laugh right. I feel confused, and then foolish about feeling confused, because that's not right either, is it? It must have happened before my job ended, but I can't remember anything specific or startling. I glanced away and when I looked back – zap. No more freckle-faced kid laughing at farts and asking will I go and play footie with him. Instead a monster, barricaded in by loud hypnotic music.

Jack grunts. Not, apparently, to my wife, who he does not hate, but to me. Now and then he tosses me an indecipherable word, usually with the inflection of a question. Hupery? Mosetier? Polikmunday?

How can I answer these?

I feel flayed. My son has plundered my life. Traitor!

When I look around my house, I see that it too has been plundered; we have not been vigilant about keeping the decay at bay. The bathroom floor needs re-tiling, the walls need re-painting, the sofa needs re-covering, the damp spot on the ceiling needs . . . something. And I am instantly, *vividly*, struck with the image of the next family who will live here. They'll gut the bathroom, first. Then they'll take our cheap MFI kitchen units and toss them in a skip somewhere. *I don't know how they lived like this*, they'll say.

But why don't we do all these things? Why can I only see other people doing them, this other family whose children will be too young to be anything but physically exhausting? We don't fix these things because we don't care enough anymore, that's the truth.

Oh well, we say.

We're at the oh-well stage.

Quite liberating, really. I blame Jack. Well, why not? He blames us for everything.

'You should have bought a decent car, not an old banger that won't stop in time,' shouts Jack when he crashes our car into a tree.

'You shouldn't have let me drive your bloody stupid new car,' he shouts when he crashes it into a ditch.

We may not be keeping the decay at bay like this other family will, damn them, but we are keeping the decks clear. We each have our little jobs, and no longer argue about who does what. I, for instance, am in charge of the rubbish. It's a man's job, and I am The Man. Six inches shorter than Jack and chronically, as they say, unemployed, I am technically still The Man. I can be trusted with rubbish, and what's more *I enjoy it*. Rubbish day is the ultimate bowel movement. Completely cathartic. Getting to the end of a tube of toothpaste, so I can make room for a fuller, neater tube of toothpaste – this gives me pleasure. The same with cereal boxes, bulky things that they are. I've even eaten cereal I didn't like, just to throw the box away. Jack, being impatient and undisciplined, opens new boxes before finishing old ones, so I have to do this end-of-box thing a lot.

Mondays might mean back to work and school for most of mankind, but for me, these days, Monday is rubbish day and therefore synonymous with domestic enema. Shopping day is the opposite and fraught with ambiguity, because the joy of replenished stores is offset by the sheer amount of stuff that now must be consumed and the remainder discarded. It seems like a lot of work. It *is* a lot of work. No, I much prefer rubbish day to shopping day. You know where you are on rubbish day.

Although lately it's been troubling me that every time I get ready for rubbish day, it seems like rubbish day was just yesterday. I watch myself lift the lids, toss in the black bags, the actions that punctuate my life, but it does not seem like enough time has passed to fill those bags.

Every day, a rubbish day.

Things like this worry me. A few thousand more rubbish days and I'll be dead.

I'm forty-five. An ancient poor sod, accuses Jack, as if this too is my fault, and if I'd only been more careful I'd still be seventeen. Contrary to what they told me, middle age seems devoid of wisdom and acceptance, and abundantly unfair to personal vanity. It is the clock ticking so loud you don't even hear it. You think it's your heart beating. Ba boom, ba boom, ba boom. It's a cruel age, cruel.

If Jack understood how being forty-five is like having a crushing social disease, would he be nicer to me? Would he tell me how he's doing, for instance? Or one day, ask me how I spend my days?

I spend my days watching telly of course. You're probably unaware daytime television is vastly underrated. There is a conspiracy to discredit it, to make daytime viewing seem naughty somehow, unwholesome, wicked. Lies, all lies, uttered by pretentious types who feel threatened by the fact they might be missing some of the good stuff. Which they are. Anyone who has missed Kilroy, for instance, cannot possibly have a grasp on modern life for the ordinary family.

'Christ Dad, *Kilroy*. That's for losers,' says Jack, but what he doesn't know is that I could easily go on one of these shows. His old dad could be a Kilroy star. My Son Hates Me and My Wife Hates Sex, they could title that day's show. I could regale the audience with tales of my seventeen-year-old accusing me of stinginess, mere seconds after I hand him a twenty-pound note. How his lips sneer when he looks at me, even though I paid for the unnaturally straight white teeth these contemptuous lips conceal. How my wife acts like she's in love with everyone else, but is so jaded with my lovemaking she doesn't even bother faking it anymore. 'Is that you finished, dear?'

My wife thinks sex is vastly overrated.

But then she thinks Kilroy is overrated too.

We are not ugly, despite what Jack says. We own our house on a nice estate, very respectable. It's a nice house, too, with a garden and swing set that used to have swings. We have two cars, both legal, and a garage to put them in. We've managed to accomplish all this, in addition to producing a healthy being to replace, well, one of us anyway. We even have a golden lab. How normal, how wholesome, how enviable can you get? We have done it! And we are still, to all appearances, doing it! Not divorced and virtually still speaking to each other after twenty-five years. Listen, I know for a fact there are thirty-eight single people just in this town, and you might be one, who look at us and think: bastards! They've cracked it!

Jack is out at a party. Some post-exam thing at someone's house, and we haven't paid much attention. We leave the door unlocked and go to bed about midnight.

At three o'clock, I wake and notice my wife is not in bed. She is in the kitchen, drinking tea.

'What's wrong?' I ask.

'He's not back yet.'

'Well, it's only three.'

'Still, I couldn't sleep.'

I think she's overreacting and go back to bed. She's always been a worrier, right from the start.

I don't remember much from those early days, but there are one or two scenes that have stayed. One winter night, waking because I am cold, to find Jack cuddled up between me and my wife. They've pulled the quilt off me. I can hear the wind screaming through the telegraph wires, and the rain hell-hammering on the roof. Maybe somewhere close, trees are falling onto unsuspecting sleeping children, roofs are being struck by lightning, fires might be licking sedate living-room curtains, flood waters capsizing boats carrying fragile cargo. *And here we all are.*

'Are you asleep? How can you sleep?' asks my wife.
    'I'm tired. That's how.'
    'You. Are. Tired.' She has this way of spacing words.
    'Uh. Yeah.'
    'Jack is out there, God knows where. And you. Are. Tired.'

Another winter's day. There's a power cut that begins in the afternoon, and goes on till the next day. No television, no CD players, no central heating, no cooking. Jack is much bigger, no more sleeping in our bed. I light the fire and candles. Our living room is shabby, but that night it looks cosy. The rest of the house is freezing. Trips to the toilet, candle in hand, are hurried affairs. We play Monopoly – one of those games you imagine you'll play a lot when you have children, but somehow, never find the time. There's a lot of laughter and I think they're so beautiful, my family. They have a purity in the fire light, a luminous quality I haven't properly noticed. My familiar worn-out wife looks mysterious in the shadows and I feel like I want to get to know her again. I had begun my adult life alone, and look who I live with! And we have managed to not injure or poison or ruin this little boy! How did we do that, my wife and I?

I sleep till she wakes me again at seven.
    'He's still not back,' she says.
    'No? Maybe he stayed the night there.'
    'I phoned the house.' Her voice is tight, like she has considered crying but decided it is too much of an indulgence and a distraction to hardcore worrying. 'They said he left at two.'
    'At two? Two o'clock in the morning?'

'Yes, that's what I just said. He left. Alone. At two.' Adding impatience to her anxious tone.

'So where is he?'

'God! If I knew that, do you think I'd be calling around asking people?' Adding hostility to her anxious and impatient tones. My wife is skilled at expressing layers of complex emotions. 'I knew something bad had happened,' she says. 'I woke up and I just knew it.'

'Right,' I say, hearing the implication loud and clear. I get out of bed, get dressed. She hovers. Paces. I put the kettle on, try to join my wife in her fretting universe. Jack! Jack! It feels like inside we are chanting his name. Summoning him in some parental psychic way.

'He could be in a car wreck somewhere,' she says, in case I need an image to get in the right mood. 'He probably took a ride with a bunch of boys who'd been drinking. Or doing drugs. God knows where he is.'

I remember Jack's birth. He's all red and angry looking. He gives me suspicious looks, that first early morning – dark furtive glances, when his mum isn't looking. He knows. I am discreetly waiting for the real father to come and take over this awesome responsibility. I am waiting for Jack to go away so I can *relax*. By lunch I feel cataclysmic love for him. It's like a physical blow to my abdomen.

At ten o'clock, I say: 'Well, I'd better go shopping. We're out of bread and coffee.'

'What? Shopping?'

'Yeah.'

'Our son is missing. Really missing this time. Jack has never not called and told us where he was.'

'Yes he has.' I'm starting to feel angry with him now. Stupid thoughtless boy!

'I'm calling the police.'

'The police?'

'You don't get it do you?'

I obviously don't. The police come and they get it. They ask for a photograph.

I remember walking Jack across the road one day, when he's about five. I look and when we begin to cross, a car zooms past so close we are pushed back by the wind it creates. If I'd started across one second sooner, we would both have been hit. Did I really look for traffic, or did I just think I looked? It's terrifying to think that not only is Jack too young to look after himself, *I am not up to the job either*.

The police ask about his friends, his habits. They write things down in their notebooks. They mention sniffer dogs in ominous tones. I sit at the table, listening, stupefied. Jack, in trouble? In real trouble? Perhaps unconscious in some waste ground? Or bleeding in an alley? And within one millisecond, my mind produces vivid images from all those news programmes. Kidnappings and murders, fatal car wrecks, and worse – the inexplicably frightening faces of missing smiling teenagers. I am not an anxious person, yet I have stored these pictures.

Jack is dead.

I will look back on this morning and remember every detail. This is how the horror began, I will think. What did I say to him last? Was I nice? Did I shout at him to pick up the towels in the bathroom, take his plate off the table? I find I have no memories at all of the last sight of my son. Nor of my last words. I look at the school photo the policeman is holding. Not a flattering photo – his goofy grin, two pimples on his forehead. My stomach feels as if something primal is leaping out of it. My wife, of course, has sensibly arrived at this terrifying place hours earlier, and she is now impervious to my sudden plunge into the abyss. Her face is white, thin-lipped, business-like. She has moved on to *coping*.

'You married the wrong person, Dad. Your whole life has been a waste of time,' says Jack when I tell him he has wasted his study leave playing Mario on his Playstation. For someone who usually mumbles, he always manages to find clarity when he has something really hurtful to say. 'It's the truth Dad, you married the wrong person.'

I've always found, and even more so lately, that truth is vastly overrated. And besides, is it true? How can you pick the right person to marry, if you don't have a bloody clue who that person will be in twenty-five years time? There may be the illusion of choice, but really all you're choosing is someone who is shaggable for the immediate future and not likely to drive you bonkers before next Christmas. Jack, genius son of mine, there is no right or wrong person for an entire life. A spouse that has grown less right is like noticing your favourite clothes no longer fit, but what the hell – they're soft, they feel good, they even let you feel like your old self occasionally. That's not to say I didn't notice that Annie Petrie from down the road, who used to be plain and boring and in love with me, has now become an amazingly attractive and interesting woman. No, these little things do not go mercifully unnoticed, but ambush me while I'm shaving or putting out the rubbish. Annie Petrie! Who would have guessed? *If onlys* taste like coffee after toothpaste. The only solution is just don't do it. Brush your teeth after your coffee.

Secretly I think Jack knows that I look at the shape of my life and suffer minute but regular panic attacks. He knows I wonder if it's too late. Will I run away, start again, be someone else, marry Annie, is it too late? No! It is not too late because I am not dead. I will do it, I will leave tomorrow, no – tonight. But probably Annie wouldn't have me, no one would, and then I'd be another sad bastard case people would invite to their dinner parties and I'd have to sit with other sad bastards. All this takes less than three seconds. I am fast at fantasy, but then I've had so much practice you wouldn't believe it. I've got a degree in fantasy.

Jack knows all this and that's why he doesn't respect me. I am afraid of Jack.

I am afraid for Jack. He would be so easy to hurt. He is alone somewhere, and probably dead. I am imagining my son's funeral, if they ever find his poor body, if I ever have to identify it in some sterile morgue, when the phone rings and it's him.

'Cannapick mupatthbus?' he grunts.

'Of course, Jack,' I say, hearing myriad doors shut on dreadful fates. 'I'll pick you up.'

The police smile, pack up their notebooks and leave. My wife has not cried with relief or acted dramatic in any way, but I can see she has begun to breathe normally again. I imagine her perspiration smelling less of fear now, less sour. She tidies the kitchen while I wonder why I still feel terrible. Perhaps I am not just slow to worry, I am slow at the other end too. Perhaps the weight of Jack's possible demise has a momentum of its own. I go to fetch Jack home. On the way out, I notice the bins are overflowing, and luckily today is rubbish day. Already.

All the way in the car, I keep saying to myself I will tell him. Find a way to tell him. It's important. I'll tell him about the rubbish days, how quickly they come round. I also want to tell him this: it used to be easy to love him and now it is not. Some days I don't even like him. But still, the fact of his existence is a daily miracle to me. If the world ceased to contain him, I don't think I could breathe.

Do you hear me? I'll ask him.

These are important things I want to tell my son.

Happy Hour

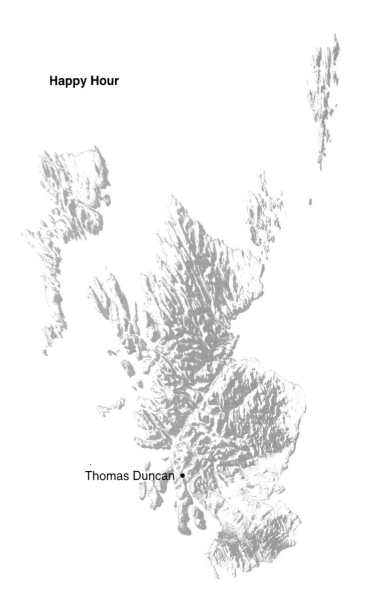

Thomas Duncan •

Ten past three in the afternoon. Through habit I commit the time to memory, then twist the key in the lock to let myself in.

Sometimes she's right there on the threshold as I push the door ajar, bursting through the tiny crack of freedom as if pursued by the Devil himself. But not this time. This time it's the stench of alcohol that charges past me into the warm August sunshine; a desperate, but doomed, bid to become one with the sweet scent of freshly mown grass. What is it about this house, I ask myself, that makes it so abhorrent to all things?

In the gloom of the tiny hallway I lean against the living-room door; hesitantly, not sure of what I'll find this time. An ill-fitting draught-excluder heralds my presence, scraping noisily across the dark maroon carpet, leaving an arc of disturbed surface dust and week-old detritus. I want to turn back, but somehow succeed in forcing my grudging feet forward into the unknown.

In the darkened room, I flinch at the breadth of domestic pollution: the toxic aftershock of Black Superkings and Black Heart Rum; the gas-fired Baxi that burns constantly, spewing out its sleep-inducing heat and carbon monoxide. I want to open the window – throw a chair through it – but I'm easily distracted, my eyes already flitting about the room in search of a long-lost stability.

I find her.

She sits, hunched on the edge of a faded floral armchair, fingers wrestling with the buttons on her beige raincoat. Although buckled tightly around her diminishing frame, the coat's open neck exposes the collars of threadbare cardigans; at least two, the sleeves of which

I know will be stuffed with tights and crumpled Kleenex.

Having no sense of decorum, or of the day's advancement, she appears at ease in pink pyjama trousers; a forgotten remnant from a succession of sleepless nights, their white elasticated cuffs falling well short of the brown suede boots that complete her ensemble. It's an Oxfam of an outfit, and one that is likely to remain intact – through entire days and nights – until God knows when.

Her thick grey hair, once her pride and joy, is wayward. I want to run a comb through it, turn back time with gentle grooming, watch as a smile returns to bless her aged beauty. But a comb is no match for this disease. Her long-lost dignity, I know, is irreclaimable.

Oblivious to my presence she sits, stooped, staring vacantly into her lap, preoccupied by her own fiddling fingers. Forcing a smile, I bow to her level and rest my hand tenderly on the nape of her exposed neck.

'Hi,' I whisper. 'And how are you today?'

She flinches, at once afraid and suspicious of this tactile greeting. In slow motion, her face turns to mine, hollow eyes loitering on my fixed smile – maybe long enough to detect the duplicity there. I'm convinced that she knows it's me, but there is not the faintest glimmer of recognition in her eyes.

She tries to speak. But her mouth, cracked and dry, can forge only silent vowels. Undeterred, she raises a slender hand in my direction, singling me out for some, as yet unspecified, undertaking.

'I want my mother,' she says, without warning. The words are emotionless, weak, undemanding, with no indication that she expects a reply, far less a miracle.

'I want my mother . . . I want to go home.'

I try to think of a response, something to console her; a different tack this time if only for my own benefit. For I know that variation is pointless, absurd even, given the circumstances.

'Your mother is dead . . .'

My father's voice. Well practised at imparting brutal honesty, he has drawled each word of his brusque broadside for maximum effect. Mercifully, his words do not trouble their intended target. But the sentiments are not squandered, seeking out an altogether more susceptible quarry, wounding me with their unintended ambiguity.

'. . . dead for forty years,' he embellishes, raising a glass of rum and coke aloft as if in celebration, but more likely to indicate some celestial route taken by the not-so-recently dearly departed. His insensitivity is due, in part, to the detrimental effect of a recent reliance on alcohol. A surprising development, we all agreed, after more than sixty years of abstinence.

'It takes away the pain of my arthritis,' he reasoned at first, latching on to the dubious medicinal properties of Guinness before citing black rum as the ideal antidote to having Alzheimer's in the home. How long before he discovers cannabis?

He looks an unlikely aggressor, my father; frail, unsteady, bloodshot eyes peering from dated Joe 90 spectacles. His face is unshaven, sparse hair uncombed. Distant days of smart black blazer and sharply-creased flannels have long since given way to ill-fitting casual shirt and urine-stained slacks, the latter being the result of a botched 'prostrate' operation. He blames the Labour Government for his misfortune. For all the world's misfortune.

'Do you think *I* don't want to see *my* mother,' he slurs, turning to me for support and understanding.

I know I should prop him up with sympathy, tell him I appreciate how difficult it all must be, put my arms around him and say, 'Don't worry, Dad, we'll get through this together.' But when did I last speak tenderly to him; touch him; brush against his naked skin? Have I ever? I am failing my father, incapable of offering love or attention when he needs them most.

Is it the heat in here? Or suppressed emotion, that makes me suffocate and avert my eyes, causing my father to seek comfort from a more reliable source: a full glass, raised to his lips and drained in one. Furtively, I draw back my sleeve: 3.25 p.m. I undo my tie and take the slow, deliberate breaths that are the essential precursor to making conversation.

'How has she been?' I ask, dutifully. I know exactly how she's been just by looking at her, but I offer my father what little of me I can, already anticipating the catalogue of complaints that are about to fall from his lips. He doesn't disappoint. I half-listen, hopefully nodding in all the right places, offering the occasional suggestion that inevitably goes unheeded.

She observes our conversation, at first transfixed in silence. Then, suddenly, beginning to offer worthy suggestions of her own: little sparks of logic, a voice of reason, sound in her mind but coming out all wrong; articulated in some unearthly language that could almost certainly be deciphered with patient coaxing.

But this background babble only serves to further exasperate my father. He ignores her contribution as being of nuisance value, and raises his voice to compete. My attempts to draw her back into the fold prove futile and are met with his fierce resistance. For my father is covetous of this conversation, our conversation, and has it under control, answering my every question, even those not intended for him.

Almost thirty minutes of his incessant chatter wears me down. It's clear that, despite the attempts of a succession of social workers and nurses to educate him in the ways of caring for someone with advanced dementia, he continues to wallow in ignorance. I ask him how he's coping. He hangs his head in despair.

'It's one hell of a disease, that Alzheimer's,' he says, understated, having read absolutely no literature on the subject. 'I don't understand how she got it,' he adds, 'she wants for nothing.' He says the words earnestly, as if expecting the disease to have shown reverence for one who lived the good life.

I make attempts to alter his attitude, explaining that circumstances will never improve, that he is not the only person who is suffering, that maybe he should accept outside help. I list the benefits of full-time care, citing a better standard of life for both of them. For all of us. But, as ever, he dismisses the idea out of hand. Blind to his own intolerance and inability to cope, he selfishly refuses to give her up.

'At least think about it,' I plead, but already his thoughts have shifted to condemnation of the weather, or of the government, or of his varicose veins. It occurs to me that my father, too, is a victim of Alzheimer's disease, but in a strictly passive sense.

Despite our obvious differences of opinion, I know he appreciates my company, but these days he would appreciate the company of a total stranger. For with friends and family either dead or discouraged, this house does not bear witness to many visitors. Only a few faithful souls continue to make the pilgrimage, but not a single one would do it for my father alone. Of this he will remain blissfully unaware until it is too late. The prospect of becoming his sole provider fills me with dread, and I pray to God that he is first to go.

I look at my watch: 4.03 p.m. My dutiful hour is almost at an end, exhausted like my spirit.

'Is that the time?' I ask, with no hope of a reply. For in this room time stands still, offering no distinction between night and day, summer and winter, life and death.

As I rise, it's obvious that my father is reluctant to lose me. He panics with the realisation that I am leaving, so he talks, and talks, about anything and everything, his open questions demanding a lengthy reply. But it's too late; he has had almost half a century to make me feel wanted, to seek my opinion, to make an effort. With fabrication and feeble excuses, I parry his repeated attempts to prolong my visit.

'I'll see you both later then,' I say, withholding accuracy.

My father continues to talk, but his voice falters as I step purposefully towards her. He watches as I kneel at her feet, my hand rising to her soft cheek as I try to get a sense of the person again. At first I am aware only of her breath, comforting, warm on my skin. But then, without warning, I feel her lips purse gently against my fingers – and my mother kisses me; a whisper of a kiss, delicate but deliberate. In a heartbeat, that precious kiss infuses me with so much unconditional love, the love of a lifetime, of eternity itself, that I fear the fragile body before me may not withstand the scale of its departure.

In that moment, I want my father to forego jealousy, to make less demands, to live and let live, to let go, to have watched and understood that even the silent can love and be loved. However, I want too much, for already he is vying for my attention, talking non-stop as if words will win the day. But the day has already been won, continually, over a period of forty-eight years. My father remains oblivious to a battle long lost.

With guilt leaning heavily on my heart, I have to leave. Out the door and out of the lives of two elderly strangers. I lock the door behind me at my father's request. 'To keep her in,' he says, and I see fit to oblige.

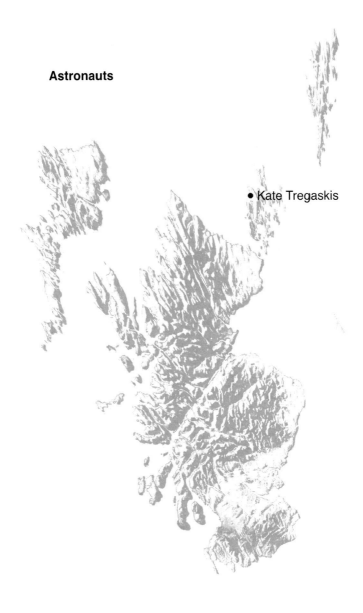

Astronauts

• Kate Tregaskis

Tom had thought of writing signs and sticking them in his window for Jen to read from her flat across the car park. But he hadn't been able to decide what to write: I LOVE YOU seemed premature; WHAT'S HAPPENING? too desperate; ARE YOU THERE? too existential. She was taking some kind of break from the relationship; in the end he'd decided to give her time. When she'd phoned last night he'd sensed something purposeful in her voice which she hadn't explained. If she wanted to finish with him, she wouldn't have invited herself over, would she? He hoped not.

It's Friday, late afternoon and Tom pushes his empty trolley around the food hall in Fenwicks: pasta and tomato sauce; a bit of parmesan; a green salad; and a nice bottle of red. And he'll need cat food. That should do it. There's a choice of tinned tomatoes. He chooses cheap, chopped. A friend who had worked in a canning factory said the chopped ones were just the pulp from off the floor, but the whole ones are difficult to break up and have a tendency to explode. Pasta. More choice. Spaghetti? It's messy but tastes better, less flabby. He'll have to go back for the veg. Why do they always put fruit and veg at the entrance?

They'd been going out for how long? Six months? Not long. They'd met at Richard's party. She was slim and practical. Smooth cool hands. Eyes the shape and colour of bay leaves. When he was near her, the world stopped spinning.

He pays and wanders out onto the pedestrianised street. The sun cuts through the crisp air, a last blast, low on the horizon. Spring. He can feel his body stirring, blinking. He puts his headphones on. Turns on the tape. The Smiths, he's just rediscovered them: *The Queen is*

Dead. He makes his way against the tide, a dizzy delirium of people peeling off their work clothes. Friday. The buses are crammed, so he walks, through Gallowgate and up between the two brewery buildings onto Westgate Road and on towards the graveyard. *Cemetery Gates* comes on, then *Bigmouth Strikes Again*. He can smell the Chinese opening for business. The smiling Vietnamese lady will be stood behind the counter; she'll spend the evening handing out carefully packed foil trays and prawn crackers in white bags. Later the trays will be strewn across the pavement, noodles spilling out like intestines. In the morning Council men will come, riding their white buggies, and clean it all up. He lets himself into the flat to the tune of *Some Girls are Bigger than Others*. No one writes lyrics like that anymore.

She should get a move on. She'd said 8 p.m. and it is past that already. Lights wink in the clumps of bubbles floating on the surface of the bath. Jen pulls the plug, stands up and wraps herself in the towel. The fact that she's left it so long without telling him makes it harder now. She hadn't meant to keep him out; she just wanted to know her own mind first. But she doesn't know her own mind. She can see the pros and cons; there are more cons than pros. Basically, it's not ideal. They get on well enough, but they never really talk about the long term. She met Tom at a party, shortly after Martin moved out. He was her experiment, to see if she could get back on the horse. But the experiment never stopped. They just carried on. One day hangs onto the next, like a game of follow-my-leader played by the partially blind.

She puts on jeans, a shirt. Dries her hair. She's hungry. Wandering through to the main room she can see out across the small car park. Tom's flat is a mirror image of her own. His kitchen window is steamed up; he's cooking something. He's making an effort then. She has never been fond of this place. They'd bought it brand new. It's a white box. She is always on the brink of leaving it for somewhere else. It was her and Martin's first home and the walls seem calcified with that knowledge. It is the box her marriage suffocated in.

Make-up or no make-up? She already feels heavy with the lines she is intending to say to Tom, already feels, through their rehearsal, like an actress. Make-up would exaggerate that and distract. Coat; keys; the wine she'd bought earlier. She leaves the flat and crosses the car park, watching where she puts her feet: the dogs use the place as a toilet. When she finally accepted that her marriage to Martin was over – they were married for just five years – she meant for her horizons to widen beyond the parameter of this car park.

Tom stands at the main door watching her. He's smiling in his socks, has been waiting for her to look up. She smiles back. In just those few days she forgot the details of him.

— I saw you coming.

He leans forward and kisses her, his lips dampening her forehead. He takes the bottle and leads her up the stairs. The door of his flat is propped open with a shoe. Apollo 11, Tom's cat, stands on the threshold, its head raised, nose crinkling. A smell of garlic and tomatoes merges with the faint smell of turps coming from the spare room.

— Nice day at the office?

She smiles at him again. The television is on. A reporter, puffed up with excitement, clutches his microphone. He's standing in front of something that looks like an airfield.

— Have you seen this? Tom nods at the TV. — The space shuttle exploded. The crew were incinerated.

— What happened?

— Some foam or something hit the wing and tore into the heat-shield . . . heat got in and fried them all.

— Tom!

— It's true.

— What does it mean?

— They're saying that funding to NASA could stop . . .

— No . . . what does it mean for your exhibition? Have you talked to Patrick?

— He phoned. You know what he's like; he reckons it's a good thing. There's still a month to the show. Enough time for public grieving to be over, but a short enough amount of time to ensure that it's still current . . . you know what he's like . . .

— Well as long as Patrick's happy. However many astronauts die and Patrick sees a sales opportunity . . .

— Yeah.

Tom turns the TV off and puts on a tape. The Smiths. Not what she'd have chosen. He opens the wine and waves the bottle at her.

— Just a little . . .

The music is insistent.

— Anyway, what about you?

She sits. The rinsed out stains and pockmarks on the velour sofa are familiar. She picks at one of the small craters on the arm. Apollo 11 jumps up beside her and pats at the loose threads with its paw, trying to animate them.

— Here . . .

He hands her a glass and sits down next to her; there's a hole in the toe of one of his socks.

— . . . How've you been? I didn't know what was going on.

Someone had once described the Smiths to her as music to slash your wrists to.

— I just wanted some time . . . I needed to think. We never really talk about *us* do we?

It's music for the unattached. Indulgently nihilistic . . . . She'd liked it once.

— What's brought this on? I thought you wanted no strings . . . after Martin . . .

— I did. I do. It's just . . .

Tom has moved closer, his knee touching her thigh. This was not how she had imagined this scene. She had wanted to deal with things cleanly, rationally. She can feel her eyes pricking. When she was little her dad would wait quietly until any signs of emotion had passed –

they were an embarrassing bodily function, like breaking wind. Now she doesn't know whether to trust her own tears, doesn't know if they are fake or not . . .

— What is it Jen?

The concern in his voice makes her want to howl.

— I'm pregnant . . .

It's as if Tom has been stung.

— . . . I don't know what to do about it, I don't know what *I* want to do about it.

His face has fallen.

Morrissey starts over again, mocking: *The Queen is Dead*; *Frankly, Mr Shankly*.

Tom gets up and turns off the tape player. The silence makes her feel exposed, as if a light has been turned on.

— Is it mine?

— Of course it's yours! . . . Sorry . . . it's just who else's would it be? Don't worry, I can deal with it . . . I wasn't even sure I'd tell you . . .

— What? Why not?

— I don't know myself what I want to do about it . . .

— Don't you think it concerns me too? . . .

— It's not that . . . anyway you know now . . .

— How long, I mean how old . . . ?

— I've felt I was for a week or so. I did a test on Tuesday. That confirmed it . . .

Tom gets up and walks round the room. He clutches his wine glass as if it were some kind of dousing device. He follows his glass into the kitchen and turns off the saucepans. He comes back carrying the bottle. His glass is empty. She refuses a top-up.

— How?

— *How do you think!*

— You know what I mean.

— Last time we were in London. I thought it was safe. I guess I got my dates wrong . . .

— Geez, that's some mistake to make . . .

— Oh come on . . . it takes two. It must have been the night of Robert's exhibition opening. We were drunk. I thought anyway that maybe I couldn't . . . I wasn't sure that . . .

— What do you want to do?

— That's what I'm asking you . . . what do *you* want?

— I've not thought about it . . . Jesus, Jen. I never thought that we would . . . I've no money . . . . You know what an important time it is for me. Exhibitions coming up. I need to work . . .

— I get the message . . .

She stands up, brushing the cat off her lap.

— Hey, you can't go. We have to talk about this.

— Why bother? It's pretty clear what you think.

— I'm just saying what comes into my head. It's a shock . . . . We don't have to fight. What do *you* want to do?

The thing is, she doesn't know what she wants, or even who she is. Nobody tells you how quickly your body changes. Her breasts are sore. Her head is awash. Her tears threaten again . . .

Tom is stood beside her now. He touches her arm lightly.

— Look, let's just talk about this. Neither of us has to do anything we don't want to do. I'm hungry, I can't think straight. Let's eat, then talk . . .

She stands in the kitchen doorway; his hands tear leaves off the lettuce as if tearing clumps of hair off the head of a doll. He rinses them under the tap. She thinks about patting them dry in a cloth to save a watery salad; instead, she watches him put them dripping into a bowl.

They eat at the small table in the living room against the window that looks over the car park. Tom has kept the curtains open even though it's getting dark. They are reflected in the glass, as if they are on a cinema screen: *our hero and heroine brood over a tough decision*. Tom heaps salad on his plate; she takes another sip of wine. Her reflection is more attractive than she is, has smoother more luminescent skin, eyes and mouth which are more pronounced, a haze of hair that dissolves into the background. She looks at Tom. Salad dressing dribbles down his chin. She and Martin tried for a baby. She hasn't told Tom this. It was a last resort to save their marriage. When it hadn't happened, it seemed to confirm that their marriage was dead.

She can see the window of her own flat. She forgot to draw the curtains before she left; it stares blankly at her, a blind eye. She feels distant from this scene, as if she were looking back on it from the future. If this is in the past, she doesn't know where the future is. She would like to get a decision made, fast forward. Get the pregnancy over, the child born, if it's going to be born, get it out of nappies, its first day at school, Tom softened by fatherhood, with a paunch maybe. Seems too late to get rid of it, it's already part of the future.

Tom dreamed of his father; his presence lingers like a smell. He wants to tell Jen about it but she's left; the place in bed beside him is cold though there's still an impression on the pillow and a long stray hair where her head was. The sun streams through the curtains. It must be late. He gets the old dressing gown off the back of the chair and goes through to the kitchen and yesterday's mess. Apollo winds herself round his ankles mewing. He forks food into her dish and turns on the radio. The space shuttle disaster. Four men and three women. The families had been waiting on the tarmac. Debris scattered over a hundred-mile radius. Trophy hunters are being discouraged from collecting the pieces, they could be radioactive.

He drank nearly two bottles of wine last night; Jen only had a glass. The empty bottles bleed red stains on the counter. He puts them by the bin. His memory is broken up, like ice floes rubbing against each other, squeaking. . . . So he's a father . . . . At least a would-be father . . . . How old does a foetus have to be to confer fatherhood status? . . . .

Except he can't be. He knows that. He's not the right kind of person. Coffee. He needs a bloody coffee. Bugger. He just wants to get on with his painting. He has a month before the show. Everything needs to be finished. Bugger.

Still in his dressing gown he sits on the stool in the spare room, clutching his coffee. The portraits he's been working on are propped up against the wall. Most are finished. There's a double portrait of Neil Armstrong and Buzz Aldrin. The two smiling astronauts look old. Nowadays they'd be eligible for early retirement. He's interested in the relationship between the two men. Everybody knows about Neil, because he was the first and he made the speech. Do many remember Buzz?

The studio is tacked with photos of the earth from outer space and of the moon, and men in romper suits, their heads enlarged by helmets as round as the back of a skull. Umbilical cords attach them to the ship as they dangle in space . . . . Bugger Jen, there's no way he's ready to be a father.

He makes himself another coffee. It is black and oily, too hot to drink. He looks over at Jen's window, parallel. What signs would he write this morning? PISS OFF maybe, or I'M NOT READY FOR THIS or simply HELP! He turns on the tape player. Morrissey again, he sings along: *I Know it's Over*; *The Boy with the Thorn in His Side*. The coffee feels like it hollows him out, like bleach down a drain. It makes sense of his insides. What was woolly and formless is now taut and oiled. He needs to eat something. He doesn't fancy toast. Cereal? OK. Cornflakes? Yep. A fried egg? No, not eggs . . . he doesn't want eggs.

The Chaddur

S. Akhtar

The years passed with varying speeds. In ten years of marriage she produced three daughters. No son.

The first two daughters, Seema and Salma, had been born in her pind. Her childhood home was welcoming, the villagers looking forward to the birth of her sons. No one had warned her of the pain. The first time she had thought she was going to die. Surely no one could endure this pain and survive? She had borne it for two days; starting with no warning, low in her back, building in slow waves. Her back had felt as if it would disintegrate, each disc unwilling to pass on the pain until her spine, conversely, was as solid as a rock. As a child she had once watched a dam being built. Dynamite had blasted the rocks until the water had flooded and gushed past the debris, sweeping away anything in its path; the building of the dam seemed to her to have created more havoc than any previous flooding. The labour pains seemed to have a similar effect on her body, leaving her weak, making her beg for the merciful release of death.

The daie, who had also attended her mother, had been bracing in her manner towards her, chiding her for not being a dutiful wife, daughter-in-law and finally daughter, all the while shaking her head and muttering beneath her breath when she thought that Khurshi was dozing. There were worried whispered conversations, where the wisdom in summoning damat-saab to be with his wife was debated. Then, after what seemed an eternity of her bearing down with nothing to show, her daughter Seema appeared, looking up into her mother's face.

Salma's appearance two and a half years later had been almost uneventful in comparison. From the moment of her birth onwards, she seemed apologetic at her lack of masculinity and tried to efface herself from notice.

Shamshad had been born in vilaet.

Her husband's cousin had been enticed overseas to vilaet by the seductive promise of being wanted; the Empire needed him and promised fabled wealth as a reward for hard work. After a few months of hearing how well his cousin was doing, Salim could not bear being left behind and he too departed for Scotland, settling eventually in Glasgow. However, Salim found living with his cousin and enduring bachelor cooking an unacceptable hardship, accustomed as he was to Khurshi attending to even his unvoiced needs. So he sent for her and his two daughters. The others thought this an act of a sentimental fool, as this was a temporary situation to be tolerated until they had made enough money to enable them to return home.

Shamshad had been delivered in hospital by staff that spoke to Khurshi loudly as if pain stopped your hearing. They gave her injections, which made her feel as if she was disembodied. She still felt the pain but she could not feel herself. Both she and Shamshad emerged from the hospital dazed, as if the whole experience had happened to someone else.

But all of that was in the past.

Salim was ambitious; having three daughters was to him a burden. Instead of enjoying the here and now, he mourned the future loss of monies. The drain of providing dowries in the future made him parsimonious in the present. Whenever new immigrants came to the city he opened up his home to them, renting out a spare room, making Khurshi provide food at a cost to the visitor. Khurshi burned with shame; this barter of hospitality went against her upbringing and she registered her disapproval by making Salim take the money. Her own parents were renowned in her pind for providing hospitality to any traveller or visitor to their village, making them welcome, giving their best even if it meant that for the rest of the month they lived on daal.

From the start Amjad had been different from the other guests.

He was from her village. A couple of years younger than her, she could just about remember him sitting cross-legged on the ground, carefully copying the lessons master ji was writing on the board. His parents had high hopes for him. The only son with six sisters to provide for, he had always been serious, taking every opportunity that came his way to improve his situation. Knowing that he had responsibilities spurred him on; he saw education as a way out of the pind.

Khurshi had stayed at the village school till 8th jamat. Her love of reading and learning had made her beg her parents to allow her to continue; her contemporaries had left joyously, not seeing the relevance in education when their skills at home-making were the ones that they would be judged upon. However, Khurshi had had secret ambitions to be the replacement ustaani when master ji could no longer teach. But that had been before the rishta with Salim came and her parents took the safe option of having a son-in-law provide for their daughter's needs.

Amjad brought her the gift of her family and childhood by recalling shared memories such as master ji's disgusting habit of getting rid of phlegm by a prolonged fit of coughing and then spitting to one side, narrowly missing where the children sat. This deplorable habit, when shared years and miles later, became a source of merriment.

Massi ji, widowed young by the upheavals of partition, who lived on the goodwill of the villagers, had sent a chaddur for Khurshi. Even though Amjad had protested that he did not know if he would ever meet her, he could not convince massi ji of this, and she had been right, they laughed. Wise massi ji, who loved all the children as if she had borne them all from her own womb. The chaddur would protect Khurshi, she was in a strange land, and her izzat and the pind's was not to be left uncovered.

At first the habit of sitting with Amjad in the evening and talking of past acquaintances and friends was a simple assuagement of homesickness. Khurshi would be knitting a jumper for Salim or hemming a new dress for one of the girls, Amjad keeping her company whilst Salim worked the late shift at the factory. The hands that had refused to till a field now regularly fed a furnace its daily quota of steel. Amjad reawakened Khurshi's sense of fun and she enjoyed the opportunity of being herself.

Amjad was homesick too and talking to Khurshi, a girl from his own village, helped to keep the loneliness at bay. Despite being a mother of three girls, Khurshi still retained that elusive spirit that had made him remember her long after she had left the pind to live with her husband's family. At first her teasing questions reminded him of his sisters, but gradually that feeling changed.

The circled 'for let' adverts grew less and less and he gave up looking for his own place despite the fact that Salim saab took almost half his wages in rent and food money. Amjad took to hurrying home from work, particularly on the nights that he knew Salim was going to be working late. At first he justified his behaviour by thinking he was only looking after Khurshi out of a sense of duty, protecting his village's izzat. But gradually he stopped thinking up reasons to excuse his behaviour; on days off whilst the girls were at school, he persuaded Khurshi to explore the city with him.

One time they took a bus to the Botanic Gardens and Khurshi grew animated at being in the warmth of the Kibble Palace, the tropical foliage reminding her of home. She had not known that a place in Glasgow could ever have the heat of her homeland. The sultry warmth was intoxicating and she wandered, paying rapt attention to each plant and tree, and in her excitement she grabbed at Amjad's arm frequently to draw his attention to a particular blossom or tree.

Amjad enjoyed seeing the plants but he gained the most pleasure from the sensation of touch. The first time he held her hand was in the park grounds as they walked down a path; it split into two and with only the slightest of hesitations he took hold of her hand to draw her down the path that he chose. There was only the smallest of delays before Khurshi acquiesced. They spent the rest of the morning not talking, each acutely aware of bare skin touching bare skin, the intimacy of fingers intertwining, the subtle pressure that each exerted to keep the other's hand within grasp.

Khurshi was convinced that her shameful behaviour must show in some way and that Salim would know that another man had touched her. But Salim did not notice anything amiss; as long as his clothes were washed and ironed, his meals presented to him promptly three times a day, and his daughters appeared well looked after, he was content. His physical needs had always been paramount over emotional needs. He watched benignly as Amjad teased Seema that she was growing sooo pretty that soon he and Salim bhai would have to set up barricades against all the boys that would be knocking down the doors in their haste to carry her away in their doli. However, it was Khurshi that Amjad was looking at as he teased Seema.

Another time they visited the Fossil Grove in Victoria Park, where the flowers all around her made her feel like a film star: Asha Parekh to Amjad's Dilip Kumar. But that was dangerous thinking and so she banished such thoughts. She managed to excuse away the look of admiration in Amjad's eyes as only the unaccustomed sunshine sparkling through.

The closeness between Khurshi and her tenant had not gone unnoticed. The excursions of just Amjad and Khurshi had been seen by both Auntypaniwalli and Auntynumber9 and much gossip had ensued with shaking of heads and a mixture of poor Salim bhai and that fool Salim, with the prediction: no good will come of this.

Khurshi, whilst always being pleasant, had never encouraged the other women to be close friends. She confined her Salaam Alaikums to the street and did not invite the other women to visit. She disliked the habit that the women had of always walking in and out of each other's homes. Seema had confided to her that her friend Nina's ammi had an endless stream of visitors, much to Nina's disgust. And so there was no one to warn Khurshi that the road she was travelling was leading to only one possible destination.

But Khurshi did not want warnings; the guilty pleasure that she enjoyed on the trips to discover Glasgow was becoming increasingly necessary. She began to anticipate when she could just be herself with Amjad, and developed a habit of looking at him from slightly lowered eyes, the veil of lashes concealing her emotions.

The first time they made love was not after an excursion but when they were at home, planning a trip to Victoria Park. Khurshi loved visiting the park; seeing the flowers and then seeing the fossilised trees made her feel alive. Salim had been home for lunch and had returned to work. The girls had also returned to school following lunch. Amjad had been on a day off and was waiting impatiently for her to finish her chores.

A storm had came from nowhere, changing the sky from a light blue to a heavy dark blue with an air of expectation. When lightning forked the sky and the rain thundered down it was almost a relief. Khurshi had gone into Amjad's room to close his window, knowing his habit of leaving it open. He had walked into the room to find her gazing at the sky, oblivious of the rain coming in and soaking her. It was like a scene from a Bombay movie: Khurshi with the chaddur, a fine muslin, clinging lovingly to her curves, not covering her modesty but inviting Amjad's gaze to linger, to explore, to touch where it touched.

They made love, inspired by the sky's passion. As lightning struck the sky, Khurshi felt that it went through her, freeing her to feel. Once they had admitted their mutual passion it became a hunger that could no longer be ignored. They made no false promises. They did not think of the consequences.

When the letter came informing them that dada ji, Salim's father, was dying, it was a shock. Salim's friends rallied round and he had a plane ticket and his suitcase packed almost before he had time to absorb the news. His father had rallied initially at his son's return, the first in almost seven years. However, he had been too ill and no drips or injections could keep him from his destiny.

After his death, the land he left behind became subject to dispute. Salim stayed on to fight for his inheritance. The months passed. Writing had never been easy for Salim and letters with their empty pages only made him uncomfortable, and so communication between husband and wife became desultory, as Salim's stay in Pakistan grew protracted to almost eleven months.

In Glasgow Amjad had continued to stay, growing more and more accustomed to having Khurshi and the girls all to himself. When he came home from work, Seema and Salma ran to him, greeting him eagerly, searching his pockets for sweets. Massaging his legs as they had done for their father when he complained of feeling tired. In return, he took them to the swing park, pushing them on the swings tirelessly whilst they entreated higher, higher, their laughter ringing out their joy. Shamshad, the youngest, even slipped up at times by calling him Daddy. Khurshi would colour up and chastise Shamshad, but Amjad looked fiercely glad and a smile would hover on his lips.

However Amjad was not Daddy. Amjad was not her husband. Amjad left as soon as it became obvious that all actions bear consequences. She, of course, had no choice but to carry on as per normal. When she did go out she wore massi ji's chaddur to protect her izzat. But mostly she kept away from everyone, knowing that some suspected, not knowing what else to do. The need to keep indoors had been instinctive, Amjad's betrayal had bit deep, and she felt as if the lightning from the storm had struck her again, this time burning all feeling from her.

The letter informing her that Salim was coming back next week was a shock.

This time, she gave birth to her son at home; luckily her pains started whilst his sisters were at school. She managed alone, not crying. She gazed at her son, like all mothers, thinking him perfect. She put him to her breast and allowed him to suckle for a few minutes. She pulled him away to kiss his face. He cried, lamenting the loss. She gave him what he instinctively sought and allowed the tears to flow

69

as she held him to her breast tightly. When he moved no more, she wrapped him in the chaddur and walked to Victoria Park to where the flowers and fossils lay. She buried him swiftly with no ceremony.

She stood at the window with the drapes drawn; she no longer cared to see the sky when Salim returned bearing news from home and gifts.

Fins

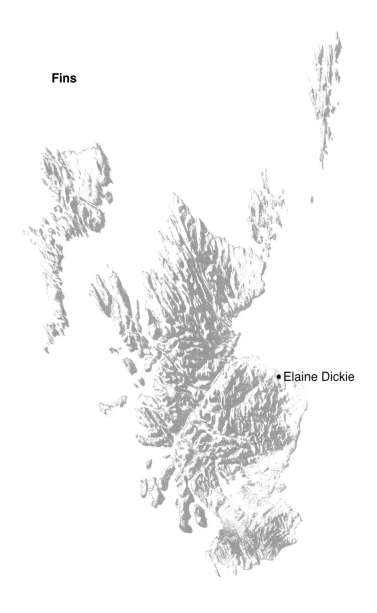

Elaine Dickie

Turquoise and aquamarine flooded into Laura's dreams. She awoke gasping for air – arms flailing in an uncontrollable breaststroke. She sat upright and slumped against the iron bedstead, feeling it dig into her back – cool metal soothing sweat-soaked skin.

It was happening again. For the first time in years, the drowning dreams were back. Electrocuted senses. Heart thudding through her eyes. Warping sound. Panic shooting out of her limbs like gunfire. If she'd been diligent, she would have expected this. If she had read the signs and taken heed, she might have been prepared.

Fluid had been masquerading as darkness and lapped around her as she slept, poking frothy fingers deep into her ears and up her nostrils, slinking silently through her closed mouth.

But then the real horror – gold and orange iridescence sweeping past her face. Black, beady eyes. A hint of warm blood underneath gossamer.

She climbed out of bed and opened the window on the far wall, letting the draught spill into her face for a moment. Her lungs greedily sucked the chill of night into every crease and crevice, expanding to full capacity before releasing her breath in a steady gush.

Darren lay unmoving and silent – unaware of her troubles – oblivious to the torrent of fear that had just spurted across the bedroom – his chest rising and falling with ease, like mammoth gills.

Laura returned to his side, and pulled the bedclothes around her. She felt her heartbeat return to normal as she snuggled into the heat of the mattress and watched him sleep. At first he looked tranquil, but soon his eyelids were pulsing and blinking in spasms as if his eyeballs were swimming around his head looking for an exit.

As she gazed into his face, he let out a snore, sending a saliva bubble to the edge of his lips. As it burst, she closed her eyes and tried to avoid confronting her horrible suspicion that she was actually in bed with a trout.

Laura's anxiety had taken years to materialise. After all, that fateful trip to the park had happened when she was only three years old. The little pond had been sparkling in the summer sun, enticing her away from watchful eyes. She had taken the chance when her mother bent to tie a shoelace and ran to the edge of the still waters. Just below the surface, there were hints of colour circling and subsiding – orange, yellow, brown and black moving silently, but occasionally sending air bubbles dancing to the top like soap suds. She was hypnotised by the silent kaleidoscope and reached down to get a little closer.

That was when she had fallen in and nearly drowned. A passer-by had heard her mother's raw scream and helped to pull Laura out. Apparently, she had been almost blue and her rescuer had to hold her by the legs and pound her back to empty her lungs of the grey murky water. Laura couldn't remember any of that, but she had one abiding feeling that left her shuddering in dread if she let it enter her consciousness – *the feeling of fins brushing her skin*.

Although Laura's dalliance with death had been a momentous event, it became buried in the past and life went on pretty much as usual. Her mother accepted her dislike of tuna sandwiches without as much as a raised eyebrow. Her aversion to keeping tadpoles was nothing remotely concerning and despite the fact that she refused to go swimming with the rest of her class, Laura's exam grades were good and she left school as a seemingly well-balanced girl, heading straight into a promising position in the bank.

As the years went on, however, Laura had a faint impression that something wasn't right. In the deep of the night, she started to feel that she had slipped through the atmosphere into algae-smothered

Atlantis, where water and fins waited to pounce as she slept. Wafer-thin angelfish stared unblinking at her, their organs visible through transparent wrappings. Thousands of tiny tangs and neon tetras zipped around her feet, fluorescent green, as if lit by minuscule lightbulbs. Clownfish and catfish loomed like hooligans and yobs.

Sometimes, the gurgle of a river, or even a dripping tap, could send a torrent of adrenaline surging through her. The mere sniff of a fish and chip shop nearly pushed her over the edge on several occasions. Her panic days started to emerge like great whales from the ocean, popping up over the edge of her subconscious and into her day-to-day life.

She thought she was going mad.

On panic days, supermarkets were particularly traumatic. Whilst meat was cut into neat squares or minced into ribbons and presented in cellophane-wrapped packages, the fish were given their very own counter. Shoals of cod and haddock were fanned out on rocks of ice, garnished with pretty pink prawns, the centrepiece inevitably a full-size prize-winning salmon, complete with Mona Lisa eyes that followed her up and down the aisles as she scuttled away, desperately looking for a vegetarian option.

Restaurants became a no-go area as chefs became increasingly creative with their seafood dishes. Menus were invaded by armies of monkfish, red snapper, herring, sole, plaice, kippers, sea bass, turbot and halibut. It seemed there was no end to the variety of species swarming around her – it was all very alarming.

On one particularly regrettable night out, just before she had met Darren, her friend Ruth had set her up with a blind date. John sounded very nice and they met up at a bistro in town. Things were going well until a waiter sauntered up to their table. John ordered sashimi of grey mullet, oyster and scallop, followed by sea bass served with a fishstock coulis. From that point, Laura couldn't concentrate on a word the poor man said. She wriggled and shifted in her seat and tried to avert her gaze from his plate.

As the meal progressed, his lips seemed to mould around his food with increasing protrusion and Laura almost ended up in a hypnotic stupor as she watched him chew and swallow. At the end of the night he drove her home and then made a move to kiss her. She felt as though she was being attacked by a giant lumpfish, trying to adhere to her with rubber suckers. Panic-stricken, she made a run for it. Needless to say, John didn't call again.

Laura didn't feel able to confess to her nameless affliction, so she kept it quiet most of the time. Only her closest friends and family were aware of her sensitivities, but she suspected even they would have found it hard to understand her unease when the highflying world of finance became infiltrated by Goldfish.com.

Even Christmas brought a new and unexpected horror in the shape of Bigmouth Billy Bass, a plastic fish that, at the click of your fingers, would flap its tail fins and sing 'Take me to the River'. It was all the rage, but her festive cheer was totally extinguished that year.

When she met Darren, things seemed to calm down. He started working in her department at the bank and, as luck would have it, they shared the same tea breaks and lunch hours. Darren was clean cut and honest looking, with beautiful earthy brown eyes. She fell in love – head over heels into his net – and glided around on a wave of serenity – elegant and untroubled.

Night drowning and panic days disappeared completely and Laura felt that all that business was in the past, that it had simply been stirred up by her mind as a way to plug a gap that Darren now filled. Yes, her life had been lacking and now things were perfect. Laura slept soundly for months.

But slowly, small things started to happen: a leak in the gutter sent rivulets past her bedroom window; a mobile fishmonger suddenly appeared every Friday at the end of her street; world fish stocks made headline news.

These were the signs that she should have taken note of before aquamarine and turquoise almost smothered her as she slept. Instead, she had been naive and unprepared and now Darren was turning into an alien trout in front of her very eyes.

Over the weeks, Laura became a virtual insomniac as the threat of overnight submergence floated in the evening darkness. She kept vigil as Darren slept, to ensure that they didn't fall victim to an aquatic attack.

Darren had been working long hours. He had risen up the ranks in the bank to the position of Inspector and to celebrate he booked a Caribbean holiday for the two of them. At first, Laura was delighted. Maybe if she relaxed and loosened up she could keep her feelings at bay and return to normality.

But even though she tried to look forward to the holiday, the thought of long days on the beach with the ocean fizzing around them began to worry her.

She hadn't been to the seaside for years – couldn't bear the thought of being at the edge of the land, at the seam of substance and water, for fear of drifting off. She kept her thoughts to herself though, and felt vaguely reassured by Darren's six-foot sturdiness; she was sure neither of them could possibly float away or succumb to the threat of liquid.

On the beach, Laura stayed under shade, reading. She devoured mountains of books, immersing herself in characters and plots – keeping the sound of the crashing waves away through the mere power of thought. But when Darren emerged from the sea, dripping with cool salt water, her stomach turned. His hair was smoothed flat on his head and a touch of sunburn on his left arm had started to flake and go a little scaly, giving him the look of an amphibious being. He bent to kiss her and the texture of his balmy skin against her cheek filled her with dread.

He never seemed to be dry; despite the searing sunshine, Darren's skin was permanently damp and dewy with the texture of an eel. He started to spend more time in the sea than out and Laura had to ignore the desire to inspect him for webbed feet at every opportunity.

The more he swam, the more she read. When she had finished all her books, she started doing crosswords. Dozens of puzzle books became filled and discarded. On the fifth day of the holiday, Laura discovered that the hotel sold British newspapers, so she rose early each day to buy them all – her knowledge of current affairs had never been so extensive.

Soon, it all caught up with her though. The trickle gained momentum and like a monster surf, it rushed in from behind and swept over her head.

The report was on page four of the Sunday supplement. The 'Frankenfish' had a single primitive lung that apparently enabled it to live on land as it walked on pectoral fins in search of new aquatic hunting grounds. Officials believed someone dumped them into the nine-acre pond, where they survived and multiplied. So far three had been hooked by local anglers. The first, measuring eighteen inches, was thrown back after being photographed. The second, measuring twenty-six inches, was killed. The third was the size of a golf bag. It got away. With a feeling of foreboding Laura scanned the ocean and located Darren sliding in and out of the silken surface like a predator.

The fish had been identified as a northern snakehead from China. With a torpedo-shaped body, snake-like head, large teeth and razor-sharp scales, she prayed he wouldn't swim into her slumber and devour her completely.

Bruised Fruit

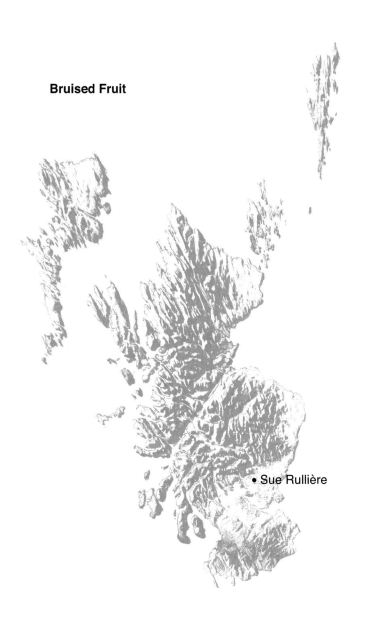

• Sue Rullière

'Take this, Monsieur,' said the woman. 'I can't go back in there . . .'

Her face was a hollow mask, drained of blood. She was holding out a knife.

Jean-Baptiste walked back up the hill from the village. He knew nothing of the woman or the knife; all he was aware of was the heat of the sun, stabbing at his back. He paused every few steps to steady his breath and wipe his brow.

The old man's bag was heavy. He'd bought sun-ripened peaches at the market, Roquefort and goat's cheese, olives with herbs, apricots, grapes and a Charentais melon. The usual weekly purchases, carried in his head but still pencilled on a list by Arlette through force of habit. He'd exchanged handshakes and answered enquiries into his health. All was well, he told them; there was life in him yet.

It was the garden that kept Jean-Baptiste going. Coaxing food from the earth was his *raison d'être*, a passion that filled his days and shaped his seasons. They were plump, his tomatoes, aubergines and pumpkins: full of juice and colour and the flavour of the soil. Jean-Baptiste had once dug potatoes too, but the ground was harder these days, his back less strong.

He kept a few sheep on his small piece of land, talking to them as he fed them, calling them by name, and sending the lambs away one by one, as a matter of course, to be slaughtered.

Arlette was in charge of the red geraniums in earthenware pots. She watered them in the early morning, when the front of the house was in shade. The excess water trickled out across the paving like dog pee, waiting to be dried by the turning sun. When the bread van blasted its horn at the gate, Arlette shuffled down the still-damp path with coins in her hand. She made salads from oozing red tomatoes, roughly chopped, with olive oil and garlic. She gathered warm eggs from the hen coop and beat them into rich yellow omelettes. When children and grandchildren were expected for lunch, she wrung the neck of a chicken and let the blood drain into an old green bucket in the vegetable store. Flesh ready for roasting, she said.

The couple rose with the sun, did their set chores and ate at set times. Only on Sundays did they change the routine and let the church bells draw them to Mass. They kept an eye on the weather, felt the age in their bones and talked only of the present. Life leaned less heavily that way.

It was a long walk up the hill in the heat of the sun. The bag was growing heavier, its handles digging grooves into Jean-Baptiste's fingers. The old man's body sagged like a waning sunflower: head bowed, weary, past its prime. Although home was not far, he stopped by his neighbour's fence, in the shade of a lime tree, and rested the bag on the ground. The air around him pulsed with the singing of crickets as he flexed his aching hand. With a neatly folded handkerchief, he dabbed sweat off his brow.

It was then that the woman's voice cut through the shimmering haze. Sharp. Urgent. Calling his name. Jean-Baptiste looked into his neighbour's field. Madame Poincet was rushing towards him in her sleeveless apron-dress and flat brown shoes.

'Take this, Monsieur,' she said. 'I can't go back in there . . .'

Her face was a hollow mask, drained of blood. She was holding out a knife.

The bag of shopping crumpled sideways and a peach rolled silently across the hot gravel of the road. Arlette would notice the bruising and would ask for an explanation.

Jean-Baptiste took the knife from Madame Poincet's trembling hand. She was pointing to his neighbour's garage. Her eyes told him what to expect.

The garage door was open. Jean-Baptiste stepped into the darkness, gripping the knife, steeling himself. He kept his eyes to the ground. Shapes formed in the airless gloom: a coil of garden hose, a stack of tyres, a clutter of paint pots and tools. Beyond them, two metal crutches lay in the dust. Jean-Baptiste didn't want to raise his gaze. He didn't want to see what he knew was there. But his eyes were used to the dark now; there was no excuse.

He looked up and saw it. Hanging, misshapen, unmoving. Like an overgrown chicken left to bleed.

A coldness crawled up the old man's back and over the top of his head. He stepped unsteadily forwards, his breathing loud in the dull, still silence. The body was suspended only just high enough, feet barely off the ground. The face was turned away. Jean-Baptiste knew the dark trousers and the creased grey shirt. He'd often paused from his digging and watched his neighbour pick plums from the trees, climb ladders to re-tile his roof and jump into his van when a building job came his way. And he'd watched him play with his son.

Louis must be four or five by now. His mother had left Monsieur Cadet a few years before, on the coldest day of winter, taking with her the baby and all the warmth from the house. So said Madame Poincet, who used to clean there twice a week and still helped out when she could. Since then, the boy only visited in the holidays.

The father doted on his son, you could see that. He played football with him in the field, using plum trees as goal posts. On market days, he jogged down the hill with the boy on his shoulders, returning with food and sometimes a toy. One day, he'd bought him a shiny red tractor. Jean-Baptiste had heard the boy's squeals of delight as his father pushed him round and round, faster and faster. And he'd seen the child at the end of the day, with a bucket of soapy water, washing down the tractor until it gleamed.

That was how things were before the accident.

Jean-Baptiste's heart tightened at the thought of the child. He stood for a moment, taking shallow breaths of the stale, stuffy air. Then he reached out a hand, slowly, and touched his neighbour's leg. Pushing gently, he made the corpse turn towards him on its rope.

The leg was cold. The expression was cold. Unseeing eyes stared out at him and cheeks sagged round a gaping mouth. 'Monsieur Cadet,' Jean-Baptiste murmured, shaking his head. Still the formality, even in death. Even more so in death.

He turned away, wanting to get back to the sunlight, to leave the darkness behind. But he couldn't. He had to stay. He had to cut the body down. Doctor, *gendarmes*, fire brigade – they'd all take half an hour at least. He couldn't leave his neighbour hanging there like that, with no dignity. Never mind what Arlette would say.

She'd have watered the geraniums by now. She'd have bought the bread. She'd be sitting in the kitchen peeling vegetables, her skin moist with perspiration.

Jean-Baptiste dragged a stepladder alongside the body. Shakily, he climbed up and put an arm around the corpse, steadying it against his chest, suddenly intimate. As he sawed at the rope with the knife, every muscle was tense, braced for the surge of weight.

The rope gave way. The body slumped. The lifeless bulk pressed down on the old man, who fought to keep his balance. Letting go of the knife, Jean-Baptiste staggered off the steps, his arms locked around the torso, the lolling head cushioned on his shoulder. He was breathing hard and his heart was drumming in his chest. Beads of sweat fell from his brow onto the dead man's shirt. Struggling to hold him, trying to be gentle, he laid the corpse down in the dust, on its back, with the collar of rope still tight around its neck. He crossed the arms over the chest and did what he could with the legs. With thick, rough-skinned fingers, he coaxed the eyelids down over the staring pupils.

The knife lay by the corpse like an instrument of crime.

As an afterthought, Jean-Baptiste unfolded one of Monsieur

Cadet's arms. He placed two fingers on the workman's wrist. He knew it was pointless.

Monsieur Cadet thought life was pointless. Pointless since he'd crushed his left leg under a ton of concrete. No one knew quite how it happened, but he'd spent four months in hospital and would never walk properly again. He moaned with pain when he thought he couldn't be heard, said Madame Poincet. He'd had no insurance, had received little compensation and couldn't work any more, *le pauvre*.

Rumour had it in the village that infection had set in and they were going to have to amputate. Rumour had it that Monsieur Cadet was suffering from depression. Rumour tends to exaggerate, Jean-Baptiste reassured Arlette.

In the gloom of the garage, Jean-Baptiste glanced at the dead man's legs: one slightly shorter than the other, and not quite straight. He took the handkerchief from his pocket and laid the damp cotton on the dead man's face.

Louis' red tractor was lying on its side in the dust. Jean-Baptiste hadn't noticed it before. Looking around, there was nothing else Monsieur Cadet could have used. He must have kicked it away with his good leg as the rope took his weight. A man must be desperate, thought Jean-Baptiste, to use his son's favourite toy. He righted the tractor and brushed off what he could of the dust.

Arlette would be worrying, wondering where he'd got to with his cheese and his melon and his other bits and pieces. She'd be imagining a heart attack in the Place du Marché, next to the flapping hens in their cages. People gathering round with shaking heads, clucking and tutting, blaming the heat. She'd be expecting a phone call.

The sunlight stung Jean-Baptiste's eyes as he emerged from the garage. The heat pricked through his shirt to the skin on his back. Madame Poincet was sitting in the shade of the doorway, with the mask of her face in her hands.

'I must go now, Madame,' said Jean-Baptiste.

His shopping was hot from the sun. He stepped out into the road and bent down stiffly for the peach. Unable to resist, he sank in his teeth. The warm juice ran down his fingers and seeped into the cuff of his shirt. The old man took his time, savouring each mouthful, drinking in the flesh that melted like honey on his tongue. Only when the stone was sucked bare did he drop it by the side of the road, where its sweet-sticky surface attracted the flies.

Better a bruised fruit than no fruit at all, he thought, as he made his way home.

Merchant City Ghost Walk

Maggie Anderson •

Summer nichts I follow the tourists tae the Glasgow Necropolis up bi the auld cathedral. They walk in groups, lookin roon, uneasy. They stare at graves o tobacco lords, big tombs wi metal bars an the statue o John Knox up on the hill. They wonder aboot the children o rich men dyin young. If they see a ghost will it have smallpox scars? They feel that I'm there, but they canna see me. Some look sad. If they come fae hereaboot they talk wi pride aboot the stane-built past. Ithers dinna care. They want tae get back tae the lichts an music at the pub. The guides tell them how evil it used be doon there in the Merchant City at nicht. They tell them aboot the ghosts o murderers, thieves, grave robbers an unhappy rich folk. I want them aw tae know why a lassie like me, fae the streets o eighteen hunner an somethin, canny rest quiet in a grave.

I had a faither once. He an ma mither had come fae the country. He sometimes got work wi the cairt horses, sweepin stables an the like. She knew dairy work, but the milk came tae Glasgow in cans on horse-drawn cairts. She never milked again. She told me country stories, an sang me the songs she used tae croon tae the coos. We lived in a wee room in a high, stinkin tenement till ma faither went as a sodjer. He never came back.

Then ma mither had tae take in men tae pay the rent. Ma brither an me slept in the close tae keep oot her way. We used tae get wee jobs. He did deliveries for the shops. I washed pots in the kitchen at the Trades Hoose, an sometimes got a meal for free too. Then oor mither took ill fae the men. Sick an tired o the pain o it, she refused tae go tae the hospital. She said they'd pit her away. She wid never tell me whit she meant. When she died ma brither took the hoose. He pit me oot.

There I wis on the street – just roon fae where I worked. I'd watched ma mither, an I knew how tae fin customers in the gloamin an the dark. It wis easy there. The businessmen knew me bi sicht. There wur Weavers an Maltmen, Coopers an Fleshers, an them, as used tae be Blacksmiths, that caw themselves Hammermen. That's a joke. They wur mostly poor souls that had too much food an drink. They had big bellies an no hammer that a girl could feel. They talked aboot aw the money they gave away tae the poor. Richt enough, they looked efter the folk who worked for them. Street women like me had tae earn every penny.

I got a share o a room in Virginia Street wi a pal. She an I worked hard nicht efter nicht oot in the street. A customer back tae the room made us mare money than one up a close. We took turns on the auld mattress. We got tae know the times the men wur at their meetins. We had oor regulars, an sent them hame cheery tae their wives an weans. We gathered a wee bit o money an hid it unner the floorboard. We wur savin up tae get new claes an bits, so as we could try for decent work in the fruit mercat or mibbe a shop. It wis hard tae keep oot the way o rough men who wanted tae 'look efter us'. Girls who didnae let themselves be protected bi them got beaten an robbed. We wur lucky, for a while onyway. It wis oor well-aff customers that kep the hard men away.

Naethin kep ma idle brither away.

When I fin I had started a bairn I went richt away tae auld Meg in Cowcaddens. She pit one o her famous seaweed poultices up hard inside me. I had a terrible bleed, there, in her shop. She charged me extra for that, an sent me hame packed wi rags. I got a ride in a cairt wi a man who remembered ma faither. He knew where I'd been. Mibbe he'd seen lassies like me there afore. I wanted tae die fae the pain in ma back.

Jeanie, the friend I stayed with, thought I wis done for. She never left me till the blood stopped. Then we got back tae work. We had tae – the rent needed payin. Ma damn brither had stolen aw oor money.

He'd pulled up floorboards till he fin it. I wis too weak tae dae ma usual. That wis tae take him roon tae Granny Black's for a drink, an then pay him in kind. I'm sure it wis his bairn I wis carryin. But for the pain an the blood I wis glad tae be rid o it.

So we wur back on the streets. We did well again for a while. The sodjers wur there wi money in their pooches, gettin ready tae sail tae India an Affganystan. I liked them. Sometimes they had pipes an fiddles, an they wur great at dancin. There wis one lad that I saw only the once. He paid me, gave me good money, just tae have a walk an a blether. We went aw the way doon tae the Green bi the Clyde. He talked aboot mountains, an white saun bi the sea wi blue islands. He said his sister, mibbe he wis talkin aboot his sweetheart, had red hair like mine, an I thought he had a voice like ma faither's. Sodjers wur no supposed tae go wi street women like us. The polis wur oot in force. Just ma bad luck. I couldnae run. I wis nabbed an cairted intae Duke Street Prison wi a dozen ithers. Jeanie wis there already.

Enter the doctor in his smert frock coat an tile hat. He had his nurse woman wi her silver-buckled belt, a fancy head cloot an her swingin redlined cape. She carried the big cauld tube that he wis goin tae push intae each o us. They shaved aff ma red curly hair, no just fae ma head either, an I didnae care whit they did efter that. That mornin we'd paid for buckets o watter, Jeanie an me, an oor hair had been washed shiny. Noo it wis lyin, hers wis gold, in the filth on the dirt floor o the prison. A warder gaithered it. She'd get a good price at the wigmakers.

One bi one we had tae lie on a table, skirts ower oor heads, drawers in hauns. I closed ma een when they washed richt up inside me wi carbolic. It fair stings when they pour it in. Some o the ithers screamed, but I never said a word. The nurse worked the tube for the doctor tae keek intae each o us. He saw bad in us aw. He said I had the clap, so I wis chained bi the leg tae the ithers.

Next mornin, efter a nicht on the foul prison floor, we had tae walk, barefoot, in a rattlin line, past aw the respectable folk, up the hill fae the prison tae Rottenrow. The prison warders knew that Jeanie an me wur pals, so we wur far apart fae each ither on the chain. Bi the time oor feet wur torn, an legs givin way, we reached this tenement. That's whit it looked like, but the close door didnae open. It wisnae real. There wur nae windaes tae the street either. Folk wid pass the place an think it wis just anither hoose, though they couldnae see in. We had tae shuffle oor sore an bloody feet roon the back, straight intae a hospital wi rows o beds. They closed the door ahin us. We wur in The Lock. I'd heard o it, but I'd never met onyone who'd been in an come oot again. Women just disappeared fae the street. It looked ordinary so naebody asked ony questions.

They told us we wur dirty an a danger tae men. They wur goin tae clean us. We had tae give up oor evil ways. We'd nivver get oot till we promised we'd no offend again. I'd promise onythin just tae be free, but I wis feelin real sick an glad o the bed an the bowls o good porridge. They took us aff the big chain an we each got oor ain, just lang enough for walkin, worn ower big broon socks an boots. I could hardly staun fae the loss o blood fae ma feet. They never healed up richt. Somebody told me the only way oot the place wis either tae the Magdalene, where you did washin an got religious instruction, or tae the Madhoose. She said we'd get mercury baths an we'd go loony or die. I asked the nurse if there wis a hospital the same for the men too. She said they didnae need it.

They took away oor clothes. When Jeanie complained the Matron said we'd get them back when we deserved them. We had tae wear dresses an drawers made fae broon cloth, hard like tattie bags. They wur big because the nurse woman had rags, soaked in nippy purple stuff, that she packed intae us. I felt as if aw ma inside wis on fire – couldnae piss or hardly walk for the pain. She tied a big bandage roon like a wean's nappie. There we wur, waddlin aboot, cleanin the hospital an doin the washin. Jeanie wis real cheery. She aye tried tae make us laugh, said we'd get oot soon. I remembered that I'd heard men laughin aboot the ducks in Rottenrow. Now I wis one o them. We never quacked.

We greet at first. The screamin came later.

The ither cure wis the mercury bath. Aff with the chains, boots an big hard drawers, oot wi the smelly rags, up ontae the widden slats, skirts kilted roon oor waists. Unnerneath us the big bath o shiny, runny metal wis heated. The smoke o it wis tae go up intae us an clean oot aw the filth. We had tae breathe it too. A highlan lassie said she'd seen the sheds where fisherwifies laid oot the gutted herrins in rows tae be smoked. That's whit we wur like.

The herrin wur wholesome. We wur filthy-dirty an bad for men. Whit aboot them? Wur they clean an healthy wi their families an servants in big hooses in Pollokshields? Whit did the doctor say tae the Hammermen's ladies when they wur sick? I never met ony o them at the mercury bath. Ma mither had been bent ower. She had sore bones an her nose wis bleedin an breakin up. She died screamin. They dumped her oot at Sighthill in the auld leper-colony grave. There wis naethin left o her for me tae visit. I wished she wis safe, at rest, away fae the men, unner a stane in the Necropolis, an I wis there too, tucked in cosy, beside her. But that's a place for rich people, no street folk like us.

Four teeth fell oot, an ma hair never grew efter the shavin. Ma skin just fell away in bits like fish scales. There wis aye this awful taste like rusty nails in ma mooth. We dribbled like weans nicht an day. Oor broon dresses wur aye wet at the neck an we aw had skitters an headaches. The nurses said we wur bein cleaned, but the stink o us wis vile.

Then Jeanie started tae scream at nicht. I held her in ma arms an stroked her head. I patted her back where there wis still some skin. Aye she cried an groaned. When she couldnae eat for yellin, they took her away tae the Madhoose.

Two young lassies came in beside us. They'd been used tae clean sick men. Some folk think that virgins, the younger the better, can cure men, but that canna be richt. Poor things. They wur raw an sore inside, cried aboot their hair an their teeth. They itched an scratched. They just wanted hame tae their mammies. We tried tae make a garden for them tae play, oot at the back. We planted some seeds an wur watchin them grow. The wee souls died afore the flooers came.

I couldnae eat. I just wasted away, but never went mad like Jeanie. I don't remember how or where I died. I know they took me down an laid me on the big stane slab in the basement. Jeanie an me had once been sent tae scrub it, but we'd no got rid o the broon stains an awful stink. The doctors wur there with their student lads aw roon. They wur talkin aboot the mercury cure. I could feel ma rotten, naked body unner a sheet. The pain an bad smell had gone an ma mooth wis clean. One o them lifted the cover. Anither pushed a sharp knife intae ma belly, slicin me open. That first cut let me go. I floated up, past them, tae the ceilin. I watched as they took ma body apart. They wanted tae fin oot whit their poison had done for me. They said that the evil sickness wis gone. Aw agreed that they had cleaned me.

They washed their clever hauns an left, shakin their heads, bletherin aboot the buts an the howevers. Not a one said, 'Stop! Enough!'

I knew then that I wid never fin a place tae rest.

She Is

•Valerie Thornton

She is the tip
missing from the finger
of the kentia palm

and the holes
in the shoulder
of a T-shirt or two

and the odd profile
on one wooden leg
of the kitchen table

and the thread
of faded scars
on the skin

and the bright wail
of the elder cat
in a new night.

Being Leonard Cohen

• Sarah Rauchas

When I was growing up, my mum and dad – and especially my mum – would say to me: 'You're living in a world of opportunity, you can be whatever you want to be. No longer are there expectations that a girl will become a housewife, or a secretary. You could be a doctor, an architect, an astronaut.'

I think they were secretly hoping I would take to law. My brother was earmarked for medicine, my sister was going to be an accountant, and they wanted a full house; something they could boast about at weddings and bar mitzvahs. But there was never any pressure; they always stressed: 'whatever makes you happy.'

My first ambition was to be a farmer's wife. Not a farmer, mind you. This was before my feminist leanings kicked in. I gave that one up when the romance of being up at 4 a.m. to milk the cows and collect the eggs was overcome by my teenage years and a liking for staying in bed till midday. This behaviour was accompanied by a penchant for desperately sad songs, which I would sing in my unique – unique because I can't hold more than one consecutive note of a tune – and melancholy way. I can still hear my sister banging on my bedroom door, asking me to please please stop, her friends were refusing to come round and visit anymore.

Then I decided I would be a psychologist. Not because I liked the idea of helping people, or because I thought it would be interesting to learn how the emotions worked. No. I had been to a careers talk, where a clinical psychologist had told us how much you could earn just listening to people ramble on about their innermost thoughts and feelings for an hour at a time. The figure flashed before my eyes; I think it was bright pink neon, with gold spangly bits around the zeros. I knew which career was for me.

As you do, I started my degree, at a university with a good reputation. I spent the first year finding myself, and the second year losing myself. By the time I got to the third year, deep and meaningful conversations – late at night, naturally – about the 'inner child' and 'the conflict between id and superego' were wearing thin and actually becoming somewhat cringe-worthy. Besides, Freud was a woman-hater and most of the rest of them were sexist men; what was a feminist doing, aspiring to prop up a world like this?

During that third year, I found myself reading Spanish poetry and speaking French. The former was not so surprising, after all, Lorca was a superb writer. But the French! Well, I can be described as the very opposite of a Francophile. I hate their films (with a few notable exceptions of course), their food is a nightmare for any self-respecting vegetarian, and their view of women is probably even worse than Freud's. What was I doing, speaking their language? Then I noticed that my accent was rather unusual. French people couldn't understand me, though they knew what I was saying if I wrote it down. It took a little while, but I did figure it out. I was speaking French with a Canadian accent. I started dreaming of Montreal. This too was odd, since I'd never set foot in North America.

Clearly there was a pattern beginning to emerge here. Probably more obvious to you now than it was to me then – my self-awareness was still quite distorted after all of that looking within myself stuff that I'd experimented with so gaily as a student. A passing comment from a friend was what turned the light on for me. He said, and I will always be grateful to him for this, 'You're so depressing!' and it all fell into place.

Once the blinding realisation came to me that I wanted nothing but to be Leonard Cohen, I quit the degree. I had things to do. I had to sell my stereo and go to Greece. All I could afford was a package holiday, a week in a self-catering complex in Mykonos, but it was a start. This, finally, was the start of my right true career. I just knew it was, I could feel it, it all finally made sense. It was a double whammy too – Leonard Cohen was the Canadian Bob Dylan, and so being the Scottish Leonard Cohen would probably also include the Dylan title. I'd always loved Bob.

It wasn't going to be easy; the training would be tough, but it would be worth it. Finally, being Jewish in Edinburgh was no longer going to be the pointless frustration it always had been. I mean, have you ever tried to find a Kosher deli outside of Glasgow? A decent piece of gefilte fish? You should have seen my excitement when they opened the kosher shelf – a whole shelf – at the Cameron Toll Savacentre. Now, after all these years, the reason for my Jewishness had become apparent; and best of all, the nose would finally be useful. Not terribly attractive, yes – that would never change without expensive surgery – but useful at last.

Probably the hardest part of the apprenticeship was the smoking. Given that I had always been a militant anti-smoker, in fact quite a little Hitler about it, I had to take a lot of ribbing from my friends as they watched me cough and choke my way through those thousand cigarettes. But I had to do it, and I was dedicated enough to carry it off and successfully become quite addicted.

I also needed to join a revolution. Cuba was long gone – a great pity since I quite fancied a visit there, it seems like an interesting place – and so I took the next best compromise. Armed with my new nicotine habit, I joined the WRP. Or was it the SWP? Whatever. I joined, I got my card, I became a revolutionary, and I left. Hit and run; in and out; did it. I've always been goal-orientated. The only trip I got was a week in Skegness, for the annual conference; a far cry from Havana, it's true, but I did get arrested once, for my involvement in accepting stolen goods – from a pensioner who had relieved Safeway of part of their chocolate stock, in the interests of socialism, and thought we needed feeding up.

One of the bigger advantages of the training was having all of those women lusting after me, adoring me, exploding at the very mention of my name. I had to learn to appreciate this, respond, enjoy – and then move on. Leave the broken-hearted angels behind me. I took to it like a duck to water; it was wonderful. I'd always found women beautiful creatures, and here I was, actually obligated to act out my deepest desires. All in the name of advancing my career. Plus I was equipped to do the job. The whole Leonard Cohen package, the look, the sound, the mystery and the *tristesse* – oh, and those black clothes – these were guaranteed to make women putty in my hands. Well, something in my hands anyway. Something extremely pleasant. I can tell you that Suzanne is a lovely woman, just lovely. Perhaps still a tiny bit annoyed about the way her whole life was invaded by that song, but a very elegant and confident person. I would have liked to get into the Nico obsession – I've always had a thing for her – but sadly I embarked on this career too late to include that in my practical work.

There were men too. Admirers who wanted to imitate my success. Wanted to write those books, live that life of exotic adventure, sing those gorgeous songs – and who wouldn't: *Beautiful Losers* has been hailed as Canada's first postmodern novel, even sometimes called prepostmodern. And I know that some of the men desired me too. Not many were prepared to actually admit that, but I could tell. You just can, can't you, and after all, I was fast becoming the master, an expert in matters of the heart, and the flesh.

Once the training was over, and I had qualified – become Leonard Cohen, fully paid-up (and there was even a swearing-in ceremony) – things changed. I found myself consumed by horrible depression from time to time, and compelled to write songs to exorcise it. The songs themselves, well they were quite beautiful, but the feelings that inspired them were not.

To add to the gloom, many many people did not recognise the beauty in the songs. They said the songs were themselves depressing.

I even knew one person who would play her Leonard Cohen albums at the end of a party, when the guests had outstayed their welcome. You can imagine that this response did little to lift the shroud of blackness that had always been hovering in the background. It had been there since kindergarten actually; since that existential crisis when we went on a school trip to see the dinosaurs at the Science Museum. Aged five, and faced with a skeleton – which they assured me was a 'real' skeleton – I just had to ask what had happened to its skin. The answer I got forced me to confront my own immortality. Now that dark shroud had become a fully present and most unwelcome guest at all of *my* parties. I just had to write these songs, but doing so was anguish; and while I thought the creations were worth that pain, they were described as 'music to slash your wrists to.'

I looked for comfort in many places. Scientology, religion, meditation. Zen and the Tao te Ching. Well, at first that was to get some credibility with the Dylan contingent, but I did find it helpful in its own right, and found myself more and more drawn to it. At one point I checked into a Zen centre, desperately in need of some healing. A kind of Betty Ford clinic for the emotions. I thought they could help me kick this habit, this addiction to despair. But after a while I found the life too rigorous, too severe, and broke out, jumped the fence in search of wine and women. And song.

To be honest, after that, there were times when I wondered if this career choice really was the right one for me. A job's a job, sure, but when it makes you this miserable, you really should think about leaving.

There were other things. I mean, have you ever tried to get car insurance? You phone around for a few quotes, and they always ask that one question: 'Occupation?' I would, naturally, say 'Leonard Cohen' – it's part of the job to deal in truth, no matter how unappealing that truth might seem. There would invariably be a pause . . . and then the voice would say 'Em, please would you hold, madam, erm, sir, while we transfer you to another department.' A few times I tried 'Bob Dylan' – this did after all feel legitimate, I wasn't exactly lying, and I knew that Bob was quite popular – but I got the same response: a transfer to the department of silence.

Still, I stuck it out. I think I had no choice really. This was what I was born to be, and the burden of that misery was my inheritance. I was good at my job, really good, and there has to be some satisfaction in that. I became a bit of a philosopher too. Over the years, I learned how to deal with the anguish, and found myself writing the occasional poem that could even be called joyous. I was more and more able to live out the conviction that had always kept me going: the certainty deep within me that there is beauty to be found in even the most tragic of circumstances.

Well, here I am now, my ambition realised, at the peak of my career, but also at the end of it. Perfect at my job, but I'm unemployed: there is just no call for Leonard Cohen these days, especially now that he's come down from the mountain. While he was in the monastery, during the latter half of the nineties, I was in great demand. People were terrified there would be no more concerts, that the bird on that wire had sung its last note, and so I was extremely popular. Could get into any restaurant, couldn't move for the party invitations.

They even started an Internet newsgroup dedicated to talking about me, loving me, worshipping me. My modesty prohibits me saying more. But that's all changed now. Why didn't I decide to become Elvis? There are plenty of jobs for Elvis. Still, at least I'm happy. Well, maybe not *that* happy, but who needs happiness anyway? I didn't sell out, and the journey was fun. And I have tried, in my way, to be free.

The Morning Ritual of Siegfried Potter-Gore

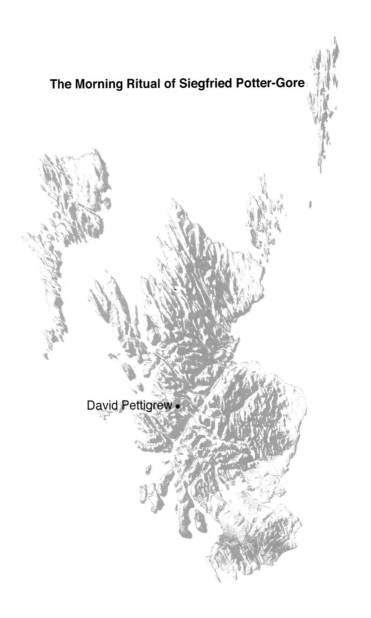

David Pettigrew •

A man of fastidious habit, Siegfried Potter-Gore wakes at 5.30 a.m. precisely. The date is Thursday, 1st of February 1945, and, as Honourable Member for Old Sarum and Parliamentary Under-Secretary to the Minister of Munitions, he has prepared for what he expects to be a busy day by allowing himself a doze of exactly five and three-quarter hours.

It is still dark in the bedroom and Potter-Gore has slept alone. However, he knows that when he reaches out to press the switch of his bedside lamp, the first thing he will see is the large portrait of Cordelia, his deceased wife, hanging above the fireplace. Beautiful, haughty, forever forty-five – the portrait captures her in evening gown and pearls, her dark hair gathered above her ears, her pale face wearing that look he used to dread. He turns on the light and black eyes dart towards him as she sits forward in her chair, aggressive, as though about to launch herself from out of the painting. But this is no more than he has come to expect and on this occasion he returns the stare for a full thirty seconds. He then greets her in the same manner he allowed her when she was alive, muttering 'Slut,' as he switches his gaze to the alarm clock.

The clock reads five-thirty-one and forty-two seconds, leaving just over eight minutes till breakfast. Under the cover of his quilt Potter-Gore rubs his belly, and finding that the cord of his pyjama trousers is loose, his hand slips beneath it. He masturbates with vigour, and while doing so visualises the cantilevered breasts of Mrs Borthwick, his typist, protruding firmly over the keys of her Remington. Her fingers batter on the machine and abruptly his vision shifts to the paper stuttering from the roller. On it there are blocks of text and numbers arranged in a list. They start with the smallest first: 2, 13, 14, 45 . . .

But this isn't what he wants to see. He squeezes his eyelids tight, attempting to re-conjure the bosom, but Mrs Borthwick's fingers suddenly move faster, louder, and the numbers get larger: 773, 1,181.6, 1,477.7 – all figures exact until the last one – 100,000 – which appears underlined, with the word 'APPROX.' hammered after it. The bell on the roller rings and there is a sharp rasp as Mrs Borthwick pulls the paper free.

Exasperated, Potter-Gore throws back the quilt and sheets. He gets up, running his hands through grey curls, and takes his dressing gown from a hook on the door. At the washstand he splashes his face, shaves, and pats himself dry. Concluding his ablutions, he plucks his teeth from a glass and slips them neatly between his gums.

It is now five-forty and there is a single knock on the door. 'Come,' he says and the door is opened by Colville, a bald manservant carrying a silver tray. On the tray is a tall glass.

'Good morning, sir,' intones Colville, bowing from the neck, 'Your breakfast.'

As prescribed by Potter-Gore's associate, Brophy – Honourable Member for Newtown Ballymagherafelt, Private Secretary to the First Lord of the Admiralty, and Ulsterman of noted loquacity – the single glass contains one very large Brandy Alexander. According to Brophy's recipe, the concoction contains much more brandy than milk, and – in respect of the War – the exotic ingredients of crème de cacao and nutmeg have been dispensed with altogether. In fact, the glass is distinctly amber, but as every gentleman knows, the drinking of neat alcohol before noon is a vulgar practice. In any case, the dash of milk helps to ease the liquor down at an early hour.

Potter-Gore ignores his manservant and takes the glass as he glides across the room. Holding the drink in one hand, he reaches into his monolithic wardrobe with the other. His habit is to leave the choice of necktie until morning and today soberness is required, so he drains the glass and selects a thin strip of black and white chequers. He returns to Colville, the brandy burning in his belly.

'Colville.'

'Yes sir?'

'Get a haircut.'

The manservant does not reply, but bows again, deeply, from the waist. Potter-Gore gives him the glass and moves to a free-standing mirror, watching in its reflection as Colville backs out of the door. As soon as it is closed, he strips, and without stopping to inspect his naked body – site of earlier disappointment – he pulls his undershorts over hairless thighs and begins to mull on the agenda of the day.

Six-thirty sharp – due at the War Rooms, Whitehall, for an audience with the PM. Or at least that was how he had described it to a circle of cronies at the club the night before. 'Sounds damned important,' they grunted, but he merely nodded with excessive gravity and tapped the side of his nose. 'Of course, gents, but you know the drill – hush, hush.' Naturally, it wouldn't do to reveal details, but timely reminders of his position keep his credit good at cards. The fact is he will not be the focus of the meeting; he is merely required to show face for his department, to sit quietly and pass the briefcase containing Mrs Borthwick's figures to a civil servant who, in turn, will pass it to the PM.

Potter-Gore buttons his shirt and sighs. If he is lucky he might get a grunt from the PM, but no doubt the old bugger will be lost in the vile fumes of a cigar and his secretary will simply offer a curt nod before sending him away. He adjusts his cufflinks and looks at the case. It sits – locked – by the side of his bed.

Ministry of Munitions: Most Secret Memorandum, No. 3041 (01/02/45). For eyes only: WSC (PM) & Commander Harris, Bomber Command. Summary, re: Bomber Command mission, 13–14/02/45. Target: Dresden, Eastern Germany. Available ordnance by this date for RAF Bomber

111

Command: 1,477.7 tons high explosive bombs; 1,181.6 tons incendiary. Equal to full payload: 773 Avro Lancaster aircraft. Detailed notes attached (see pages 10–14 for USAAF support).

Given present pop. (100,000 APPROX.) and square mileage of city centre area (details enclosed), certainly enough to achieve excellent success.

S P-G, MoM

It didn't look much on paper, but this brief memo involved Potter-Gore in considerable hardship. Amongst other things, touring the production lines of Northern bomb factories and their rows of smirking, yellow-faced tarts. He had only been in the job eight months and, frankly, it was not to be borne. The only consolation was that he might bask a little in the reflected glory of these big missions, and – true – there was a curious satisfaction in reducing the biggest raids of the war to just a few neat lines.

Potter-Gore's hand smooths down the front of his suit and he gives a brief tug at the ends of his bowtie. Checking his side view in the mirror, he watches the electric light bounce from his shoes and then goes to collect the last item of his attire, a carefully brushed Homburg which waits on the tallboy by the window. Also on the tallboy sit a polished mahogany box and matching boxed calendar. Potter-Gore picks up the calendar and twists the dial on its side to change the date. Of course, he knows perfectly well what the date is, but when a large red '1' slides into view he raises an eyebrow and says '*oh, yes*' loudly, even though he is completely alone. He sets the calendar down and his hand drifts over to the mahogany box, fingertips smoothing on the grain. He snaps open the metal catch and carefully raises the lid. Inside lie a revolver and a single cartridge.

The Webley Mk VI, officer issue from March 1915. Potter-Gore received his at Sandhurst during the final December of the War – that is, the last one – and as a Second Lieutenant with 1st Battalion,

The Buffs (East Somerset Regiment), it had more or less remained pristine within the holster of his Sam Browne throughout ten months in France. He had, of course, waved it about on a few occasions – whenever he was required to herd his men beyond the wire – but the weapon has only ever been fired once. Just once.

He picks the revolver gently out of the box and weighs it in his hand. Dependably solid, it's in near-perfect condition, the only damage being a slight scratch near the tip of the barrel. But like his shoes, the dun-coloured metal positively gleams in the light. Potter-Gore tightens his grip around the handle and assumes the firing position, ramrod straight with arm outstretched. He aims the gun at the clock. The time is five-fifty-two.

Night patrol near Belleau Wood, 1st of February 1918. Accompanied by Lance-Corporal Lang – a Cameronian recently seconded from a neighbouring division – Potter-Gore had been ordered to give the new boy a tour. Lang was a stolid creature, a lowly member of the Scotch gentry and suitably agricultural in bearing. But although enormously tall and broad, there was something cowed about this man, about the way his face twitched uncontrollably when they were introduced by the Captain. This was a mere hour before the patrol was due to begin and while Potter-Gore shook his hand and chuckled ingratiatingly about the fun they would be having, all the time he was assessing Lang's bovine frame and facial tic, calculating how far they would get before his trembling silhouette gave them away to German snipers. Ten yards, possibly; fifteen for certain. As it turned out, they managed forty before the fucking oaf lost his footing and lumbered on a mine.

Up in the air they went – noiseless, winded, the stars spinning – and when Potter-Gore came round he found himself lying on top of Lang in a shallow ditch. He could feel the Scotchman's body underneath his own, very warm, damp, the ragged movement of his diaphragm lifting him up and down as though he was drifting on a wave. At first he couldn't hear, but his ears popped abruptly, in time to catch the full force of Lang's scream, which emerged not continuously, but in panicked staccato bursts. Over on the enemy side, a sniper answered each scream with a crack from his rifle. Nearby, bullets spat into mud.

'Lang. *Shut up*,' he whispered, but Lang merely bellowed in reply. They were face to face and Potter-Gore could feel the man's spittle on his lips, smell the hot stench rushing up from his stomach. He shifted his head from side to side, but found there was nowhere to move. A flare from the sniper trailed through the sky and in the orange glow Potter-Gore saw there was no cover to escape to. The ditch was grave-width and for several yards on every side the ground levelled flatly away. Shots zipped overhead or landed left or right. The flare didn't reveal their position, but with every scream Lang was doing his level best.

In subsequent musings Potter-Gore always remembers the danger of that moment. But he never fails to congratulate himself on escaping the predicament. Lang, suffering from some unknown, ghastly wound, had screamed like the proverbial stuck pig. But it was Potter-Gore's higher breeding, the patrician coolness – hard-learned from the floggings of his schooldays – which kept his mind clear and saw him through. Lying on Lang's wrecked body, he felt no pain, but he wriggled his toes and fingers to make sure he could move. Then he unclipped his holster and drew out the Webley. Without raising his arm above the ditch and without getting mud down the barrel, it was somewhat awkward positioning the revolver correctly, but with patience under fire he manoeuvred it into place above his comrade's left ear. He waited a second or two for Lang to scream once more and when there came a last, good blast from his lungs, on the answering report from the German's rifle, he pulled the trigger and blew out his brains.

Lang was silenced, but Potter-Gore was so close to the detonation that as soon as he fired sparks seared up the right side of his face. He howled while his eye burned, and it took all of his self-control not to leap up in agony. Instantly, bullets swept over the mud and he pressed his face down onto Lang's. His colleague's final breath was rattling in its throat, a curious noise like the groan of a dog, and on the stinging area around his eye Potter-Gore felt something warm and wet. He rubbed on it for relief until, in the dim light of another flare, he raised his face a half-inch from Lang's. Dead eyes stared out, empty orbs reflecting the starburst orange of the flare. Lang's mouth was open and somehow the cataclysm of the bullet had forced his tongue out as far as it could go. It was on this that Potter-Gore had soothed his eye.

Eventually the sniping ceased, but Potter-Gore waited hours before crawling back over the parapet of his trench. Dawn was approaching and his battalion was loading up, preparing for the 'morning hate' – thirty minutes spent firing round after round at the German lines. He staggered through the crush to the entry of his dug-out and sat down, panting. The sergeant gave him a mug of rum. 'Just in time, sir,' he said and Potter-Gore grinned. The sun was coming up on a blue sky and in the first rays he saw that the front of his uniform was entirely covered in Lang's coagulated blood. From the button at his throat, down past his crotch, the green of its material had become a rich, stiff mahogany. Around him, men clattered up on the firestep and further down the Captain bawled at them to fire. The guns roared tremendously, and he sat back, drinking slowly from the mug.

Fingering the scratch at the end of the barrel, Potter-Gore is certain it was caused by the splinter of Lang's skull. He unclasps the chamber of the revolver and picks the cartridge out of the box. It slides easily into one of the six empty cylinders and he spins the chamber with his palm, repeating the action as he moves to the painting of his wife. Imperiously, she looks upon him, but he turns away, snapping the spinning chamber back into place.

For some time after the incident, Potter-Gore supposed that his embrace with Lang was the closest he had come to another human being. But this was a romantic notion, dismissed on remembering his wet nurse and the fact of his mother's womb. Nevertheless, the notion clung on, reappearing at odd, indolent moments. Finally, on the night of his wedding, he assumed it would be expelled altogether. But when he clambered onto his wife's rigid body and felt her breath on his face, he thought of the ditch, his revolver, and of Lang's corpse, solidifying beneath him as the hours wore on.

Potter-Gore removes his teeth and drops them into the pocket of his suit. He closes his eyes and puts the revolver in his mouth. The barrel is cold, heavy on his tongue; its metallic tang mingles with the aftertaste of brandy. His finger rubs on the trigger and he imagines his death. The splinter of his skull; his body released. A ruby spray for Cordelia's dress. The gun sight jars the roof of his mouth, and the hammer creaks as he cocks it with his thumb. His spine buzzes as he pulls the trigger. There is a dead click as the chamber revolves.

Moments later, Potter-Gore relaxes his jaw and takes the Webley from his mouth. He unloads the cartridge and shrugs as he wipes the barrel with a handkerchief. Outside an engine rumbles, and moving to look through a gap in the curtains, he sees that Colville, now in driver's uniform, has brought the car to the front of the house. It is still dark, but in the light shining from the vestibule, the servant stands by the passenger door, the grey of his peaked cap darkening in the drizzle.

With one minute to departure Potter-Gore returns the cartridge and revolver to their box, and places the Homburg squarely on his head. He gives a final glance in the mirror, checking his bowtie and smoothing his suit once more. His hand runs over his pocket, and discovering a lump, he reaches in. It's his teeth. He slots them back into place and grins, tapping the dentures together as he adjusts his hat to an angle over his brow.

He bends for the briefcase. Mrs Borthwick's figures feel light in his grip and his feet spring from the carpet as he strides for the door.

The time is 6 a.m.

Flying

• Kirsten Gow

She jumped you know. All the way down. From the roof of the school gymnasium to the soft ground below. Not soft enough as it turned out.

They say that she wanted to know if she could fly; to feel the upward rush of air past her skin and through her hair. And so she paced the flat asphalt roof – up and down, right to left, east to west – intently examining the rough grey surface as it passed beneath her moving feet. And we all watched, stomachs firmly knotted and rising in our throats. Frozen solid on that summer's afternoon.

Right to the edge of the roof she paced, toes of her shoes curled over the edge, the sound of collective hearts stopping as we all stood numb. Her taut body teetering for long, painful seconds, blonde hair billowing in the breeze, before she turned back to the full stretch of roof behind her. Our shoulders relaxed a little, and relief washed over us for one split second, and then she broke into that run. Our hearts racing as she ran the length of the gymnasium, speeding up with every stride. Ran for her life. Ran out of roof.

She's still there. Suspended forever in the mid-air of my memory. Arms outstretched to greet the thin breeze.

And even after the rumours of tangled limbs, after the blue flashing lights and stern assembly warnings. Even after her awkward return, bulked out by the back brace and displaying that distinctive limp, even now we still envy her.

Because at least now she knows.

The Cow Pond

Sheila Puri

There were no aeroplanes in the sky, nothing. Only the voices of the auntia, coming towards him to feed skinny cows. They asked if he'd heard from his parents and told him that he was getting thinner and that he should eat makhan. Lal said 'Acha ji,' his eyes fixed on the empty baskets held tightly against their waists and he wondered about that tightness, and how it would hurt, how they still talked and smiled as if nothing mattered. His little brother he'd carried like that, into his waist, little babu's chubby arms making shapes in the air, trying to be free and he'd had to hold even harder to stop him falling into the mud. The thought of his little brother and his parents in England sent a fist into his stomach before he remembered that they were going to call him as soon as they saved money for the air fare. The fist released as fast as it had first come. It was like that with him.

When the auntia and their baskets left, he watched cows, biting, chewing, softening dry chappatis, the bones of their backs moving all the time, stopping only after they'd swallowed the mush. Today, by the cow pond, Lal felt alone in the world. He often did after a beating from grandfather but today it was worse, because chacha Bhaga hadn't come.

He was sure everyone in the village knew about the beating. It had happened this morning after grandfather asked him to fetch milk from mata ji's house. But, in the gali, Lal saw reds, yellows, feathers and strings, flying against the sky, the man shouting balloons, balloons, balloons. The voice loud and repeating pulled him, and a fast ache to hold the magic colours, to see his fingers turn yellow and green, was in his belly. He watched them floating up, down, sideways, up again,

123

tickling him, making him want to giggle with their teasing. He ran over to be beside balloon man and forgot the milk.

'Tell me balloon chacha, what is it that makes them look like big laddoo, chacha, tell me?' he said, trying to pull one down. Balloon man smiled, Lal was the little boy with a big mind.

'A magic king on the other side of the fields blows a spell to keep them round and fat.'

'Take me there, chacha, take me there,' Lal said, his little-boy sense always wanting to be somewhere else, doing something else.

'You're going better than that, in an aeroplane, to Engaland; you can buy all of India's balloons then.'

Lal's eyes left balloon man and were with his mother's face; his eyes went to the empty space next to him where his father would have been. It made him long to fall flat on his face, to let the earth bang right into his nose and mouth. He grabbed the strings and pulled some balloons down, stamping them to the ground, making them burst, again and again, make noise upon noise, not caring about anything, his grip and pull on the string becoming harder, fingers tearing and scratching into the balloons. He didn't hear balloon chacha telling him to stop, that they would burst, they were empty, just full of air. It was only when balloon man grabbed his arm and said, 'grandfather pays first, then you do what you like' that he remembered grandfather and the eleven o'clock milk drunk after the ten-minute breathing and five-minute stretching exercises.

Lal ran to mata ji's house, all the while thinking of giraffes with iron legs and how teacher said they were the fastest animals on earth, and thinking if they were ever to look at the strongest grandfather on earth, his grandfather would have his picture in children's school books. He wondered how come two brothers could be so different: grandfather, thin and hard; chacha, soft and squidgy mal.

'Here have a drop of lassi and I'll get the milk,' mata ji insisted, 'tell this boodhi mai some of your stories.'

But he told her he was late, he'd seen balloon man and if he didn't hurry he'd be in big trouble. Mata ji understood and went to fetch the pot while Lal got the cow ready, making little sucking noises so that it would know that he wouldn't hurt her. Mata ji always said he was a good boy.

Back in the gali with the milk in his hands, he ran, not noticing the splashes over the iron glass, until dadee ma sitting with her daughter-in-law called, 'Be careful. Don't you know it's pahp to spill milk?' and added laughing, 'What will you feed your bride if you go about wasting milk at your age?'

Grandfather would hit him for spilling even a little, so he began taking each step carefully, holding the glass away from his body, making sure it stayed like a white lake.

'What you doing boy walking, lolling about like that; hurry, you think your father, that ooloo da phata's going to bring me milk?'

Hearing the words against his father, Lal forgot the milk; instead he saw a dirt-covered dog in someone's doorway, trees with little leaves, the evil-eye avoider on Jora's house, and he felt something hard against his feet. He'd forgotten to watch out for bits of dried twigs and stones and now a stone got in the way and he fell forward, the metal glass flying out of his hand, the clan, clan, clanking of it bouncing along each stone and sending white liquid in sharp lines, in curves, in drops, colouring the stones grey-white and turning the mud pale. He didn't notice the stabbing pain, or the blood or the choking in his throat. A shadow filled him, his arm burned where grandfather's hands tightened, cold air hit his back where the kurta got pulled up. Grandfather's other hand came down like a bullet on Lal's legs, back, stomach. Blinding pain blinded him, milk, steel glasses, cows, giraffes became one. Hearing the noise, neighbours rushed out telling grandfather to stop, but grandfather said he had to fix him, said how else would he learn to do as he was told, too much hanging around with that scoundrel, chacha, the good for nothing who never married, and with this another sharp hand hit Lal almost as if Lal was to blame for chacha's life as well as his own.

The world became quiet. Lal wrapped himself with layers of invisible cotton, a thick rajai between himself and everything else.

And now alone, the sun burnt into his neck. Waiting for chacha, Lal pulled off his kurta and pyjama and dipped himself in the pond, and the darkness of the pond moved up his body, stinging him where grandfather's hands had been. Only after some time did the water begin to cool him. He was glad the real heat of the month of jahait, when the pond was gone, hadn't yet started.

Beginning to feel cold he pulled himself out and sat on the earth, letting the sun dry his skin. A beelee came close to his feet, its bones sticking out of its back. Lal would have given it roti but he didn't have any. It was funny, he thought, how ooloo da phata was more of a swear word than ooloo da beelee. After all shit was shit whether it came from an owl or a cat. When he'd asked the boys in the mandi they'd laughed and later he'd tried his aunt, and she'd told him to never say these words again. Lal never knew when he would make people happy, sad or angry. He thought that if he never spoke another word, became a sadhu wandering village from village, then everything would be okay. Maybe, the sadhus too had been beaten. He decided there and then that if his parents didn't get a ticket for him and his chacha stopped liking him, he'd become a sadhu. Now that he had a plan, now that chacha hadn't come, he was ready to leave the cow pond.

The next day at the mandi, when he'd gone to use the chopping machine for the cow greens, he heard two boys talking.

'The fever's got chacha Bhaga.'

'He's old,' said the other one.

'Can't go on forever.'

When they saw Lal standing behind, they stopped talking.

Lal asked, 'What's happened?'

The older boy spoke quickly, 'Nothing, after rest he'll be okay.'

The boys let Lal do his greens first, but he still needed to get the greens home, milk and feed the cows, clean the dung, give grandfather's lassi, put the empty glass in the rasoi and only then would he get to chacha.

When he ran to chacha's, people shouted, 'Careful son, you'll fall.'

In the courtyard mata ji was placing a cloth on chacha's forehead. He wanted to say, 'Get up let's play five stones, come on time to feed the cows, hurry.' Instead he went to him, placing his head close, believing the closer he got, the more chance of chacha waking. Mata ji told him that he had just fallen asleep a few minutes ago. Wanting to do something he said, 'Mata ji, give me the cloth.'

She handed him the wet cotton and asked if he'd eaten and without waiting for an answer went into the house to make paratha. She'd seen by his face that he hadn't put anything into his mouth all day.

Alone now, he looked properly at chacha's face; it was older, paler than he remembered, like the colour of a roti that's been put on a cold tava and thrown to cows and birds because it doesn't cook properly. Chacha opened his eyes, ready to speak.

'I was waiting, son, for you.'

'Rest.'

'It's all rest, always rest for us old ones . . . there's not much time . . .'

'Don't say that, I'm going to get you better, you'll see. I'll feed you makhan and cream, I'll massage your back and head with mustard oil; you're always telling me how mustard oil cures everything.'

'Of course son, but let me give you something . . .'

'I don't need anything, just you to be well, now rest.'

For the rest of the day he cooled chacha when his temperature went up, feeding cardamom and basil water when he awoke, cajoling him to eat some kheecheri. Visitors came in and out of the house. Lal noticed the postman at the side of the bed nod his head and say, 'God has come to take him back.' Everyone said the postman was clever, he could read and write, always read the letters from his parents first to grandfather and Lal would insist that he read them to chacha. He'd agree, laughing, saying, 'Well, when you go abroad, remember to bring me an English biro.' And Lal would reply, 'Only one, I'll bring you ten.' But now Lal wanted to make him go away; he hated the postman.

Later grandfather came.

'Bhaga wake up, wake up, your older brother is here to see you. You not even going to get up for your visitor?'

Lal saw tears in grandfather's eyes. He saw others sitting by the bed, quiet, saying no to tea, water, milk; this was how it had been when grandma died.

It was getting dark; grandfather told Lal to get up, that they should go back. Lal didn't move. He said he wasn't going, that he would stay with chacha. His grandfather's eyes were fierce like hot coals. But it was chacha's life he had to save and if he gave in and went away chacha would die. He wasn't going to let that happen; looking at his feet, he said, 'I'm not coming.'

Rage filled the small courtyard. The invalid forgotten, grandfather went to grab Lal's arm and to drag him out and mata ji stopped him and said, 'Son, he'll be okay, I'm here.'

Lal had never heard grandfather called son before, he was always 'dada' or 'bapu', and he saw grandfather's face change and somehow grandfather looked smaller than before and the way grandfather turned to face chacha's bed, the way he bowed and said sri akal to mata ji and walked out the room, Lal knew he wouldn't get a beating when he got home. And in the quietness, he heard chacha.

Lal went up close. 'You are a special boy.' Lal wished he could cry.

The nights were chilly so they put twigs and pathia on the chula and heated water for chacha to give him an earthenware pot to keep him warm. When mata ji had checked that it didn't leak, Lal took it to chacha's bed and lifted the blankets to place it at his feet, but they were cold, cold and still, like stones in December. Death was cold. His nose needled, and became sore. Mata ji, her arms piled high with quilts and pillows said they too should get off to sleep, especially because they had to be well to look after chacha. When Lal didn't answer she looked over and saw Lal, still and staring.

The ten-year-old and eighty-year-old sat beside each other. There were no more words, nothing more to be done.

For days, Lal went in and through the village, just getting on with the cutting, the gathering, the milking and sweeping. When he passed mata ji's house she called out to him to come and sit beside her while she made churi. Lal wanted to be alone but knew it was rude if he didn't do as she said, so he walked into the warm dark. She gave him a stool and herself sat on a mat tearing soft chappati into small pieces, getting them ready to mix with ghee and sugar. He wondered how come she used freshly cooked chappati for churi, not like other people who used day-old chappatis.

Into the darkness she spoke.

'You know even kings and queens leave behind everything; all who come into sansar have to leave sansar.'

He sat listening. She continued.

'Bhagwan too needs good people you know, beta.'

'But, I need him.' The words came out suddenly, sharply.

Lal had said too much and mata ji wouldn't like him for being angry with God and he waited stiffly. But instead of slapping and telling him not to speak out of turn, she walked over to be beside him, placed her arms around his back and pulled him towards her thinness. He cried into mata ji's shoulder, making her kameez damp.

Afterwards, she gave him warm churi, which at first felt dry and he found hard to swallow. But the more he chewed, the more he noticed how hungry he was and he could taste the sweetness of the sugar and the softness of the makhan mix together; the saliva began to flow in his mouth.

After he'd eaten, he offered to help with making patia from the cow dung and putting them on the rooftop to dry. He knew that mata ji would need fuel to light her stove for the next day, having used up so much of her own for heating chacha's food and water.

It was when he was making these that mata ji told him that chacha had wanted the house to be sold to the landlord to pay for Lal's airfare to England.

When Lal washed his hands under the running water of the nalka the cow dung made the water run white and brown. The clink clink of the pump in his ears as mata ji worked the pump, knocking out all other sounds for him. Knocking out all confusion.

By the time his ticket for England came, it was the month of jahait, too hot to do anything and the cow pond had become another bit of sandy land and the cows wandered about the village, fed chappatis by householders and sheltering in the shade of people's homes and shop verandas. Instead of becoming a sadhu, Lal went on a train and aeroplane ride, first Punjab to Delhi, then Delhi to London, then London to Glasgow.

Glossary

Cow pond when it rains in the Punjab large puddles form where cows gather and kids play.

Auntia plural of aunty (children refer to adults as uncle or aunty).

Chacha a respectful way for a youngster to address an adult; literal meaning – 'uncle' (father's younger brother).

Ooloo da phata swearing – 'shit of an owl'.

Dadee ma elder women can be called this; literal meaning – 'paternal grandmother'.

Chappel sandal.

Rajai thick cotton quilt.

Kurta tunic.

Ghur solid molasses.

Ooloo da beelee 'shit of a cat'.

Bhagwan God

Jahait the name given to the hottest months of the year.

In the Beginning

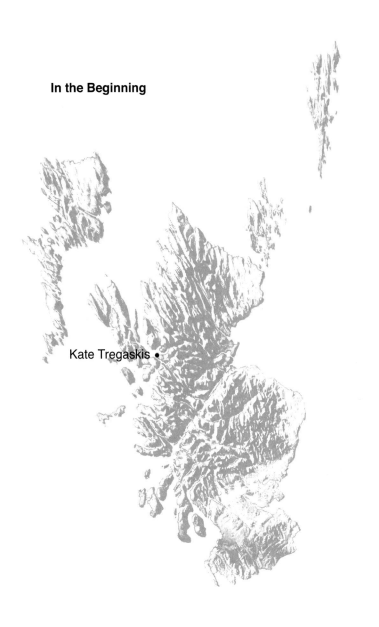

Kate Tregaskis •

The room feels close. Myrtle can smell her brothers, a sweet near-nothing smell like spit. Air whistles through Tom's nose as he breathes. It seems too soft, as if he were sipping rather than drinking deep. Baby she can't hear. She gets up to check he is OK, opening the blinds slightly. His eyeballs twitch, animals stirring under blankets. His lashes flutter on his cheek.

She's thirsty; she pads slowly down the stairs in search of a drink of water, trying not to creak them, one foot after the other reaching into the dark, the hairy carpet felt not seen, bits of sand prickling between her toes. A light shines through the grooved glass in the door to the kitchen. She slides it open, stopping when she hears her aunt on the phone.

— . . . well, the mother died. Completely unexpected.

Myrtle steps away from the door and leans against the wall.

— There were complications with the birth that weren't picked up . . . I know, poor little mites . . . she bled to death basically . . . at home in their bedroom . . . she was rushed to hospital . . . it knocked Geoffrey for six . . . well quite, as you'd expect . . . no, the baby's fine . . . six months now . . . I know, tragic . . . . Yes, well I offered to step in. He's taking a while to get back on his feet. Well, quite . . .

Myrtle sits on the carpet, her arms round her knees, her heart pulsing against her leg. She pulls the hem of her nightie, stretching and folding it over to cover her toes.

— You can imagine . . . with the school holidays and all . . . just associations . . . yes well, it's just a little holiday. They're used to it here, come here every year . . . normally they rent somewhere. It'll give Geoffrey more of a chance to put himself back together . . . well,

133

he's got to for their sakes . . . I know . . . I don't know how he'll manage . . . he never was very practical, since we were small . . . well it was his wife . . . three's a lot for a man on his own, if it was just the older two then he might manage . . . the girl, Myrtle, she's capable . . . but a baby?

Mind your own business! Myrtle bites her bottom lip; it's like a worm between her teeth. *Ruddy well mind your own business!* The blood tastes of coins; her lip stings.

— We're hoping they won't have to be split up . . . . Well no I couldn't . . . a few weeks is one thing. Exactly . . . exactly. Yes, mine are fine . . . . Brian? He's got a big job on. He'll be back at the weekend. Yes . . . yep . . . hmmm . . .

Myrtle closes the door quietly, her heart thumping. She goes back upstairs. In the bathroom the toothpaste stains from the plastic cup hurt the bite on her lip and the water tastes funny. She goes back to bed. Mummy wouldn't have wanted them to be here. She never liked their aunt, her flapping tongue, her words filling up the house like buzzing bees.

Why can't he push the pushchair? Myrtle's had it for ages. Tom reaches his hand up to the handle: it's his turn now. Myrtle smacks at his hand. She walks faster, her footsteps ching-chinging on the tarmac, echoing off the empty streets and into the clear air. The plastic wheels whisper something, but the words are one extended hiss. If she wheels Baby there, then he's going to wheel it back, because otherwise it's not fair. Baby is his baby too. A couple of gulls take off from the road. They have been pulling something out from where it has been pressed flat on the teeth of the tarmac; their long beaks easing whatever it is out. Tom looks for blood. It could be a run-over cat. He's seen one of them, with its tongue stuck out to the side, eyes like china marbles. But as they get closer, it's someone's fish and chips.

They go up the hill, cross to the other side of the street, edging out between the parked cars and look both ways for traffic even though there is none. He puts his hand in his pocket. The sting where Myrtle hit him rubs against the stitching. His shorts are too tight. Mummy would have bought him new ones by now, but she's dead. He tries not to think of Mummy dead; maybe her tongue stuck out. He wraps his fingers round the coins in his pocket. He's going to get a sherbet fountain, and three spaceships, blue and green ones, because pink is not like real spaceships, more like babies' toys, and some red shoe laces – and if he's got anything left, some blackjacks or maybe he should get some fangs or a lucky dip bag. Myrtle is Mummy, he is Daddy and then there's Baby, going to the shop. They walk past the swing park which is empty, the gate locked. When they get to the shop, the sign isn't outside and he gets a bad feeling. Too early.

Myrtle leads them back to the swing park; they walk round the edge till they come to the hole in the fence next to the bush, big enough to take the pushchair when they fold it up. They are going to play until the shop opens. His favourite is the horse as it has a real horse's head. He runs his hands over the cold contours where the red paint has been rubbed off and you can see dark metal below: the eyes bulge, its lips curl back and its nostrils are wide. With only him on the horse it is hard to make it move. It is supposed to rock back and forwards but it is too heavy on his own, even though he is standing up and pushing with all his weight. He runs to the swings where Myrtle skims gently back and forth with the baby like a big toy on her lap.

— He-llo, hello, Baby, Baby, who's a baby? He tickles it under the chin, but the pudgy face turns away. A bit of sour sick dribbles out of its mouth and it struggles and makes a grinding noise.

Tom clambers onto the next swing. He flicks his legs to power him higher and higher. Gulls clamour. Little matchstick boats, all facing one way, float on the sea beyond the rooftops. He drinks in the salty air. The high point is scary, one more push means he'll go right over, the heavy metal chains in his hands jump. He's flying. His hair flaps at his collar where it has grown long. Mummy would have cut it by now. If Mummy was really in Heaven, then if he swung hard enough he might reach her. If she leant down and he stretched up, then they could meet. He feels like his body is filling up and up with air. He doesn't like Aunt Sarah. Why couldn't they have come on holiday with Daddy and not her? *Daddy's not feeling well. Daddy needs a rest. Daddy is sad.* Daddy would feel better if he was on holiday with them. He'll buy a postcard from the shop, if it doesn't cost too much, and write to him. Tell him to come.

Myrtle's voice cuts through his thoughts. She is stood by the swing, holding Baby out towards him. He slows, bringing himself gradually to a stop by scuffing his sandals on the ground.

— Here, Tom, you take him. I need to pee. And keep a look out, make sure no one comes.

He takes hold of Baby; it's heavy. Tom sits back on a swing, clinging with one hand to the chain, the other awkwardly round his brother. Myrtle looks about, walks to the wall, pulls her knickers down to her knees and squats, her back to him. He can hear the hiss, see the dust of the playground darken in a puddle under her crouching body.

Baby begins to wriggle. Tom's arm is going numb. He'll put his brother in one of the baby swings, the ones with the bars around to stop them falling out. He finds the rubbery legs underneath the blanket and puts them either side of the bar.

— Hold on Baby.

He places the plump starfish hands on the metal and then pushes the swing gently. Myrtle is stood looking at the puddle she has made. He pushes the swing some more. Baby is making happy noises. The sun is getting more intense, notching up, as if someone is turning a knob. He pushes harder and Baby swings higher, a car goes past slowly, he can hear the suck of the tyres on the tarmac. Myrtle shouts something as he gives the swing an extra shove and watches the seat rise in the air. Too late, he sees how unstable Baby is. He watches it shift and then tumble. It lands on the ground. Myrtle is running now.

— Idiot!

Baby contracts slightly and then erupts with a full-throated howl that feels its way into the silence, getting louder and louder.

— Look what you've done.

Tom slumps against a swing; he is suddenly cold, the sun has disappeared. He can't look, for fear of what has happened, for what might have happened, for what he has done. He starts to cry, silently, his mouth open. He didn't mean anything. How could he know stupid Baby wouldn't hold on?

Baby's face is a bluey purple with rage, its features scrunched up, its nose flowing, the sound hacking at the silence. Myrtle is shuss-shussing it now. Tears, which it doesn't normally have, break on its cheeks and run down its face. Myrtle lifts it up and lays it against her shoulder patting it, bouncing slightly at the knees. On its forehead he can see where the skin is speckled with grit and blood is escaping. Myrtle dabs at the blood with spit on her hanky.

Tom's heart rams itself against his chest as if it were trying to break out. His ears roar. He wraps his arms tightly round his torso, looks at the feathery scuff marks on the toes of his sandals. Little shards of broken glass blink on the concrete, and then blur, a kaleidoscope of shining lights piercing his own tears. He wants to go home. He wants his mum. He doesn't want to be in this stupid place, with stupid Baby and his stupid sister.

— Tom . . . Tom! Myrtle is talking to him; he lifts his head hesitantly. — We won't tell anyone, OK? We'll get a plaster from the shop and put it on and nobody needs to know. We'll say he banged himself.

Myrtle spends most of her money on a box of plasters to stick on Baby's head, and some lovehearts. Tom buys the sherbet fountain and the spaceships and some blackjacks and a postcard of the seaside with a stripy sunshade and a lady in a yellow swimming costume smiling and a donkey with children on its back. It is the card he thinks will be most likely to make Daddy want to come here, because if he wanted he could have a ride on the donkey.

— Where have you been? Aunt Sarah is stood at the door looking at them. Her dress is splattered with flowers, pink, purple and brown. She is squeezing a tea-towel in her hands as if she were trying to hurt it.

— Sweets, Tom says, holding up the evidence and stepping in front of the pushchair so she doesn't swoop down on Baby. — We got some sweets. Want one?

— It's naughty to go out without telling me where you are going. I was worried. You really mustn't do that.

— It's all right Aunty, Daddy lets us go to the shop.

Tom looks at his sister, is impressed with the way that she can say things and make things OK. Myrtle takes the baby out of the pushchair and hands it to Tom.

— I think he needs a little sleep Tom, you better put him down, in our room.

Aunt Sarah looks like she's going to object, reaches out towards Baby, but Myrtle has stood up close to her, blocking her path.

— Aunt Sarah, can I ask you something? Tom, off you go before he wakes up again.

Tom takes Baby, its breathing hardly perceptible. He takes it up the stairs and lays it down in the cot. He sits under the windowsill. The multi-coloured blinds knock against the wall with a hollow metallic sound, scraping against the wall when he leans into them. He can hear Myrtle and Aunt Sarah come up the stairs, talking. He lines up his sweets in the order that he is going to eat them on the green and gold bumpy carpet that smells of feet.

When he goes into the bathroom, his sister's knickers float in the bath. They are stained with a red-brown smudge and surrounded by swirls of what looks like blood. Myrtle had told him – when he'd got out of his bed and climbed into hers because he was missing Mummy – that their mummy had bled to death. She'd said that babies come out of the hole that girls wee from and that after Baby came out,

138

blood came out too and the doctors couldn't put it back and so Mummy definitely wasn't coming back. He looks at the blood on his sister's knickers. Was it starting to happen to her too?

In bed that night the sanitary towel between her legs feels thick and awkward. Myrtle is worried in case blood will run out of her and onto the sheets so she keeps pressing it up against herself. She's afraid that if she falls asleep, she will wake up awash. She hadn't wanted to tell her aunt, but what else could she do? Aunt Sarah said she was too young. She had to speak to the lady next door who has two daughters. She had given Myrtle the pad with loops at either end and a pair of special knickers, which were too big for her.

They had been shown slides at school, the boys and the girls squashed together on the carpeted floor of the staff room, which smelt of coffee and biscuits. They had looked at pictures of a naked man and woman that the lady had called Marmaduke and Matilda. Marmaduke had ginger hair like marmalade, on his head, under his arms and around his willy which stuck out like a school dinner sausage – different from her brothers' willies which floated like little scraps of pastry in the bath. She hadn't been able to eat sausages since. Matilda was ginger too. Her body was swollen up; her titties stuck out and there was a brown bird's nest of hair between her legs. The lady had explained sex and where a man puts his thing, and about periods and about a lady who took a dog with her so she could blame it when her waters broke. The boys in the class had giggled. She had been glad that the lights were turned off and the curtains drawn so nobody could see her. None of the girls wanted to ask questions, because there were boys there and the boys didn't want to either.

She wants Mummy, but Mummy is gone. Daddy built a bonfire and burnt the sheets and other things. He hadn't meant her to, but she'd seen the blood. He had told them to stay in the house. Aunt Sarah said that Mummy bled to death, and now she is bleeding, sticky and dark, a gash on the white towel between her legs. Aunt Sarah said

139

she was a woman now, and that she must be big and strong for her brothers, and for her daddy. But her aunt is the enemy. Her flapping tongue might split the family up. She has already taken them away from Daddy. Her aunt said that it would be all right if there were two children, but a baby as well is too much. Baby has brought all the problems.

What if he went away? What if she found another mummy for him? Maybe a lady on the beach with a picnic basket and a sunshade. Or maybe they could leave Baby in a church, give him back to God. Tell God: *Thank you but we don't want him*, returning him like Mummy taking Christmas presents back to the shop because the colour didn't suit her or because she could do with the money.

Myrtle gets out of bed. A warm slug of blood slides out of her; she feels its moisture escape to the edges of the towel. She waddles to the bathroom to check the damage and clean herself up. Light coming through the bathroom window is watery. It is still early.

Tom is asleep but Baby is awake and smiles at her when she leans over him. The street outside is quiet except for the clink of the milkman's bottles and the purr of his engine as he makes his way up the street. She picks Baby up, whispering to him and carries him downstairs avoiding the creaks. She collects his bottle and lies him on the floor as she mixes up formula like the nurse showed her. She straps him inside his chair, opens the front door and heads towards town. The air is cool. She knows the town well. They came here every year, sometimes twice. Aunt Sarah needn't think she was giving them a special holiday, because this was their holiday anyway, the one they always have. When she passes the church it is black and imposing, wrapped in shadow. Baby is starting to grizzle; she stops when she sees a bench and gives him some formula. Where is she going to put him? The town is suddenly not big enough. As he sucks greedily on the bottle, a train in the distance grinds to a halt, metal shrieking against metal. She could take him to the train station.

She chooses a carriage at the far end with no one in it. She lifts the pushchair onto the train and climbs in herself, chatting to Baby to keep him quiet. Just before it is due to depart she climbs off. She has tucked his bottle in beside him, so anyone who finds him will be able to feed him.

Sunshine is streaming through the blinds; it's morning already. Myrtle and Baby aren't in their beds so Tom goes downstairs to look for them. Brian, Aunt Sarah's husband, is in the sitting room, home for the weekend. He's slumped in a chair watching TV, cricket; the ball thwacks off the bat, there's a ripple of applause. A small figure in kneepads jogs stiffly across the screen.

— Are you up then, sleepy head?

Tom doesn't speak to Brian but goes into the kitchen. Myrtle and Baby aren't there either.

— Sarah's nipped down the shops. She's getting a picnic so we can all go to the beach later. She won't be long. Do you want me to get you some breakfast while we wait for the other lazy boneses to get up? Brian stands in the doorway.

Tom shakes his head. Aunt Sarah has laid out the breakfast things. Up-ending the cornflake box over his bowl, they cascade out and over the table. He looks at Brian. Brian doesn't react so he adds milk and sugar, and sets off across the living room with his bowl. He's going to take it upstairs.

— Hey, little man, eat in here in case you spill it!

Tom keeps walking, does not look at Brian. He holds his breath and makes it to the doorway, puts his bowl down precariously on the carpet and slides open the heavy door.

— OK, have it your way, says Brian.

Tom slides the door closed behind him. The door is made of glass panels with horizontal runnels which distort whatever you look at through it. He can see Brian's large figure, sliced into stripes, move back towards his chair and the TV. There's more applause and a man's voice gives the score.

Upstairs, Tom eats his cornflakes and then gets the postcard with the donkey on it out of the paper bag. He has some coloured pens that his aunt bought him. He's going to write to Daddy. He doesn't know where Myrtle and Baby are. They might have died like Mummy. He's going to write to Daddy and make him come and rescue him.

Deer Daddy – Tom's tongue wets the tip of his nose, his hand aches from gripping the red pen – *Plees com an git me. I want to go home. From Tom.*

Myrtle opens the front door quietly. Applause and then music greet her from the television set. The house smells different. Brian is here, his big shoes are in the hall. She creeps up the stairs, elated. A weight has been lifted, a problem solved.

Tom is lying on his front on the carpet, writing a postcard. He hands her the pen and she writes their daddy's name and their address for him. Everything is going to be all right. Baby has gone on a train to find a new mummy. Their daddy will come soon and take them away and everything will be OK. She puts her arm round Tom. He seems pleased to see her.

Translating Duncan

Saket Priyadarshi

Her skin was the first to die. Duncan buttoned up her nightdress, closing off the exposed V above her breasts. Gently, he placed her arms by her sides and lifted the bed-sheets. But there he hesitated and looked down at his wife one last time. Death was a plague upon her skin.

Leaning over her, he suddenly felt a warm breath against his face. Her chest was as still as the land, but Irene was breathing. Something twitched in the side of her neck and the movement continued: engorged veins rising and falling, and rising and falling, as if her heart had just come alive. She groaned. Her lips moved. She was whispering, something like:

'*Lisa . . . . Poor Lisa.*'

Lisa? It really didn't matter. All it could mean was that her mind was still astir, even if lost in some drugged dream, in a dying vision. In fact, as far as Duncan could gather, her every organ continued to function. The water tubed into her stomach dripped out thin yellow in a bag below the bed, proof that even the kidneys showed no sign of failing, so how could they be sure that this *was* the end? Only an hour ago he had been perplexed by their certainty; but then her skin began to mottle. Sickly colours swept over his wife.

The side-room was as unbearably hot as the rest of the ward and Irene's clothes were damp with perspiration, but he did it anyway. He wrapped her up like a newborn in deep mid-winter, tucking the sheets below her chin. He couldn't bear to watch another inch of her bruise before his eyes.

Duncan heard talking outside the door. Young voices, probably the nurse saying something like: 'Not long now.'

He recognised the silhouette of the junior doctor behind the glass, nodding gravely. Expecting them to knock and enter, he quickly turned to Irene, pulled out a hand and clasped it in his own. He waited, but nothing, not a sound. Although he had not heard them come in, Duncan felt sure that he was being watched. Perhaps they had tiptoed into the room and were standing reverentially behind him by the door – a respectful, safe and useless distance away. He turned to the two sombre faces that he now knew so well, and found them not there. The door remained closed, the shadows were gone.

Irene always did have cold hands. He returned the limb he had extracted back under the sheets. Curiously, her face remained untouched by the colours. How reassuringly pale she was, her dull grey lips still bubbling, still a little moist with life.

She groaned again and he sat forward in his chair. Who wouldn't want to hear their name? But instead, yet more indecipherable mumbles. She kept repeating them. Was she in pain? Should he call the nurse? He leaned closer and listened. No, there was more to her noise than just groans. There were words, words in another language. Something-*yavitch* and so on. Foreign sounding words, and names. Was it . . . could it be . . . Russian? How immense and unfathomable the mind was! Forty years since she had last spoken that language.

Susan arrived just a few minutes after her mother had passed away, rushing into the side-room as the nurses were tidying her up. Hysterical, she was nudged and guided by an experienced auxiliary into the family area. There she suddenly fell silent, shocked by the sight of Duncan dipping a biscuit into his tea. She didn't say anything, just stopped at the door and stared. Then she called her brother Donald. He was in a meeting but would leave immediately, of course. He must have remembered to ask how his father was. *Fine*, replied Susan, *drinking tea*. After Donald, she phoned her husband and left the same message.

Irene lingered. Duncan thought that these would be the worst days of his life, but they weren't. He had imagined the first weeks would pass so heavily that a day without Irene would seem a year, but that's not how it was. Susan and the wee ones moved in. Donald announced that he would take a few days off work. He sat with his father full time, returning to his flat and his girlfriend only after 5 p.m., sometimes as late as six.

Of course, it wasn't exactly a merry time, but it seemed to Duncan that the house had held such precarious lulls before. It took on the air of one of those Christmases when everything had gone wrong. When Donald and Susan had run out of insults to snap at each other and Susan's husband had already left for the pub. When the wee ones were bored beyond pleasing and Irene had long since disappeared into the kitchen. It felt no worse than a drawn-out instalment of those awkward hours until she returned smiling with a plate of sandwiches and ideas of how to occupy the youngsters. He was fooling himself. Of course, it was nothing like that. Only – it felt as if Irene was just *away* somewhere, vanished of her own accord, invisible again in a private moment.

She lingered on the furniture she had chosen, by the walls she had decorated, in the garden she had sown. Duncan walked by her photos without stopping. He didn't really miss her. When he came in from a walk he took off his boots and stood them next to hers, still standing empty in the hall, without even noticing. No, she didn't feel distant at all. He had no need to seek her out in photographs or her possessions; she was everywhere in that house. Everything inanimate and mundane reverberated with her life – the cutlery, the stains on the carpet, the soap.

But she lingered most not in things but in the words she had left him; and above all in the startling truth of what she had said about their two children. Duncan had dismissed it at the time – morose thoughts, he had told himself, the chemotherapy. But she was right:

147

there they were behaving just as she said they would and even though he observed them with the periphery of his vision, his wife's words haunting his ears meant that he had never seen them so sharply focused. Susan couldn't do enough. The more she did the more she found to do and the more agonizing and guilt she brought upon herself. *A sufferer, like my sister Beth*. And Donald was no use at all, but each act of comforting was given like charity, orchestrated like a donation. How right she had been. *Do you love your children?* She had asked him one day, out of the blue. *Of course*, he had replied, a little brusquely. *Because if you find that you don't, that you don't even like them, I wouldn't get bothered over it. They're not children to be loved anymore.*

Twice a day, Duncan would escape the house with the excuse of taking his grandson for a walk. Robby loved the beach like a lad from the city, and ran from the sand to the dunes to the edge of the sea with the energy of a young collie, but the second day after her passing away, he showed none of his usual enthusiasm.

'Granda?'

'What son?'

'Where's Granny?'

They stopped.

'She's away Robby,' he replied staring at the islands in the west, wishing Irene would whisper what to say. 'She's . . . gone away.'

The boy turned to face the same direction and tried to look as sagely across the water as his grandfather, wondering if that was where his grandmother had gone.

The first few days after Irene's death passed quickly in his family's company, but then the business of mourning began.

An odd thing happened at the service. Near the end of her sermon, which up until then had been no more or less than the usual, the Minister seemed to say a few sentences in a different language; and no, not Latin. It sounded like . . . Russian. On hearing those strange

148

words, Duncan felt himself sinking into the pew. He was going mad. Why would she do that? His mind was playing tricks. It had been a hallucination. Or had it? Because at exactly the moment he thought he heard her utter those foreign sounding incantations had not the whole assembly shifted in their seats, slightly? Had not Susan and Donald exchanged a look? But nobody mentioned it afterwards and that night as he lay in bed Duncan thought not of the fact that he had just buried his wife, but of how he had heard the Minister speaking Russian.

Perhaps she had and perhaps everyone had heard it. Perhaps everyone who had been there was now lying awake, confused and alone, wondering if they had, in fact, imagined the whole thing. And all because it had not been the subject of the usual speculation and scrutiny that should have followed. It was like that story he had once read Robby: *The Emperor's New Clothes*. It ended with a child, oblivious to the adult fear of being ridiculed, telling the plain and simple truth: the Emperor was naked, couldn't everyone see? Either that, thought Duncan, or he was indeed going insane.

'Robby, son. Did the Minister say anything you didn't understand?'

Duncan sat on a rock watching the sun set behind the islands. Robby had lost interest in the horizon ever since he had kissed his grandmother in the coffin (Susan had insisted on it) and seen her lowered into the ground.

'What d'you mean Granda?'

'When you were sitting down at the funeral and listening to what the Minister said?'

Robby nodded.

'Did she say anything that sounded . . . strange?'

The boy shrugged. 'I don't know.'

'Think back son, 'cause if she did, I'll try and explain.'

Robby was drawing shapes in the sand with his boots.

'*Well* . . .'

'Aye, go on.'

'Why did she do that bit where she talked like how Granny used to?'

'Like Granny?'

'Aye, when she wanted to make us laugh.'

Duncan wondered how much of the service had passed him by? The shock of hearing Russian must have made him deaf to the part the boy was talking about.

'But, I didn't think it was funny the way the Minister said it. It made me scared.'

Duncan put an arm around his grandson.

'Awch, there's nothing to be frightened of.'

Robby looked up.

'Just you remember it the way Granny did it.'

It wasn't only with children. It was just as easy to reassure anyone of any age; everyone, in fact, except yourself.

To seek reassurance from an eight-year-old boy was madness in itself. Fairy tales were for the simple. Fables could be of no comfort to a man of sixty-eight who was hearing things.

Susan, Robby and his wee sister moved back to their own house some days later. Duncan insisted that he would manage just fine and he really thought that he would. The first week without her had not been so bad, but as soon as he was left alone in that house, nestled in the hillside and hidden from the road, the falling apart began. Irene was everywhere and nowhere. He felt her presence in every room, but her company in none. What was he to do? How was he to fill the minute after minute of her absence? During the last few months she had insisted on time to herself. Two hours, twice a week in fact, when she disappeared to goodness knows where. He could admit it: he had resented it at the time, thought it a selfish act; but now he was repentant. He understood. She had been doing nothing more selfish than preparing him for this phase of her having gone.

150

And it should have been no more than a phase, but with every passing day bringing a deeper gloom, Duncan became less and less sure of its transience. After all, it was not as if Irene would ever return as she had from those mysterious appointments. She had not prepared him for the permanence of her absence. How could she?

He hardly ventured out the house. Dark clouds followed him everywhere. Loss *was* a scar, a hidden wound that would never heal and one that he was ashamed to show anyone. But they all came anyway: the doctor on a post-bereavement visit; friends from the village *just passing by*; Susan with his tea; and even Donald, although he was more likely to use the telephone. Luckily, they arrived in daylight, before the hours had truly worn him down, and left before his nightly demise.

He would rise as early as ever, shave and wash almost with his old enthusiasm for a new day. But then, coming down the stairs, the silence from the kitchen would remind him. The egg would shatter in his hand or the yolk would break or, sometimes, land perfectly intact but on a cold pan, the stove still unlit. Hours of nothing until lunch time. The bread would burn and the tinned spaghetti hoops would stick to the pan. Some days he would force himself to step into the garden, but then he would find himself outdoors and wonder what he was doing there. He would leave tea brewing in the pot until it became cold and foul. Daytime television was other people's problems, suddenly irrelevant and modern – nothing he could learn from. He waited for Susan with mounting excitement but as soon as she arrived he wished her away immediately. And as much as he missed Robby, he knew he was too unsteady to be playing with children, too weak and joyless to be making up stories and running around.

One day, the Minister knocked on his door. She made the tea, not the first visitor to do that, and asked the usual questions. She did it discreetly but Duncan could tell she was inspecting the house and his clothes, his fingernails and hair looking for those tell-tale signs.

They were sitting at the kitchen table when, after a pause in the conversation, she said, 'I hope you were satisfied with the arrangements?'

'Aye, it went very well, I thought. I've been meaning to drop by and thank you,' he lied.

'And I hope I didn't say anything that might have . . . upset you?'

She was a round, little woman with short dark hair cut like a man's and a ruddy face on which she wore giant circular spectacles.

'No, no. The service was . . . just fine.'

'Well, if there's anything. I find the feedback useful.'

He examined her again. Did she know what she was asking? Duncan felt his madness rise again and insisted, a little too enthusiastically, he later thought: *No, he had no complaints or queries at all*.

Nobody called during the night and those were the most desperate hours. Susan would leave the house in pristine condition, just like her mother. The dark outside imprisoned him. He found it impossible to read. He cried uncontrollably and one night fell sobbing into Irene's wardrobe.

He had got into the habit of opening it every evening and staring at her hanging dresses, wishing he could walk through them into another world. Then, one night he stumbled as he leaned into the dark. His fall to the bottom of the cupboard was broken by plastic bags full to the brim with what he thought were letters. He picked himself up and set about lifting the bags out of where they had been so carefully stored. There were three in all and each labelled. The one at the front had a white sticker attached to it on which was written in thick black ink – *I's*; the next one, the largest, was marked *I+D*; and the smallest at the back, *D's*. Surprised, Duncan delved into the last bag, his own – *D's* – and pulled out not envelopes but a handful of photographs. They were of him from years and years ago, even some black and white ones. Had he really forgotten them? Their wedding pictures and some others were in the living room, and yes, he remembered Irene arranging an album dedicated to his parents and the house near Troon, his old school photos and even his years in the Air Force. But these must be rejects that she, for whatever reason, had kept. He knew he should have started with Irene's bag and then moved on to theirs, but he went straight to his own. It held such a pitiful collection in comparison to the others. The $I+D$ bag was by far the biggest. It was as if his and Irene's had been systematically emptied to fill it to the brim; and Duncan's had been emptied most of all.

Irene had obviously looked after these photographs well, especially her own. How could she have so many? What could they possibly show? Duncan gave up on the childish notion of looking through his own and instead reached into those of his dead wife. But what lay at the top were not photographs but sheets of paper. He took them into the light. They looked like old letters. No, not old but recent. You could tell by the feel of the pages. And when he unfolded the sheets he saw, true enough, writing arranged in the form of letters; but this correspondence was in another language. In fact, in another script altogether. There were six such letters, between two and three sheets long. On the top right margin of each were numbers: a date and year, *this* year. Between the date and year was a word, a foreign word for a month presumably, but every other word was a guess, except where he imagined *Dear* to be at the start. Who could have been writing to her? And in what language? Could this be Russian? Was it a name she had whispered in that dying room? A Russian name? Duncan shook with disbelief. Six letters hidden like this, all in a stranger's hand, not one of them signed.

The next morning he set off to walk the two miles. He was determined to look her in the eye and ask. He left the house steadfast, marching briskly, but by the time he had reached the cemetery he had been reduced to a hesitant and wary shuffle by a rising sense of dread. He stopped at the gate. Are some truths better left uncovered? He could turn around now and burn those pages but . . . . The weakness passed. He pushed open the gate and strode to where his wife lay buried.

He didn't see it for a while. The new blades of grass distracted him. How swiftly they had sprouted. Then he read and reread the message on the plaque. And when he did finally look down to examine the state of the flowers, he couldn't trust himself to believe what he was seeing: a white envelope held like an offering from fresh carnations. He stared at it for a full minute, perhaps longer, blinked hard several times, but it was there right enough. Eventually, he picked it up and opened it to find a letter, in the same script and hand as the others; and again – no signature.

He walked aimlessly along the beach with the letter in his jacket pocket, stopping every now and then to stare back at the isles. They seemed to mock him. Even the once familiar sound of the waves was now a chorus of Russian jeers. He wanted to throw the letter away but couldn't. Pathetic, weak, scarred and unsteady. The sky was darkening above him and new rain spat upon his face. He turned to begin the long trudge back, but suddenly he stopped. Duncan felt himself being watched and looking away from the sea he saw the old white cottage on the raised beach and from its open door the plump figure of the Minister, waving. She was beckoning him to come over.

The manse needed repairs and so she had been barracked out to this holiday home. *Luxury by comparison*, she whispered. The house was so cosy that Duncan almost fell asleep on the couch when the Minister disappeared to put the kettle on. He roused himself and walked over to the window where an easel had been arranged. On this, a canvas and the beginning of a watercolour of the view out west.

'I think I'm going to call it *Translating Islands*.' She was light on her feet. Only a touching distance away and he hadn't heard a rustle of her return.

'Well, it's coming on just fine.'

'It's proving very difficult. This light is so . . . well, tricky. You've lived here so long Duncan that you probably don't even notice.'

All he could think to say was: 'An unusual title.' What *was* her name?

'I suppose so, but you know Duncan when I look at the islands I think of . . . other things. I mean are those islands really as I see them or are they what I want them to be? Idylls? And that reminds me of God and the work I do and the people I meet. Is it not *all* open to interpretation?'

Duncan hurried through his memory but her name was lost. He had forgotten the Minister's name!

'Even people, even ourselves,' she continued. 'Have you ever considered it, Duncan? Are we who we think we are or who we want to be? Are *we* translations? And if not can we *be* translated, into something else, something better?'

Unable to conjure up a single word in reply, Duncan stared at the painting, feigning, he hoped, contemplation.

'Anyway, rich teas or bourbons? And no more funny talk, I promise.'

She took his order and returned to the kitchen. Duncan walked across the room to the modest bookshelf. He began at the top left but soon lost interest. They were all religious texts, to do with her work. The next shelf was the same. The third was more interesting: Austin, Brontë, and Dickens . . . . The fourth: Nikolai Karamzin, Turgenev, Pushkin – in that order – Dostoyevsky, Chekhov . . . . Suddenly the dread returned. Tolstoy! The last three books were *Teach Yourself Russian* and a pair of imposing dictionaries – Anglo-Russian and vice versa.

'Ah, someone else interested in the Russian language I see.'

Goodness knows how long she had been standing there. She was carrying a tray laden with everything necessary.

'No, no,' he denied a little too robustly. 'Just looking, that's all.'

The Minister smiled, knowingly he thought, as he stepped out of her way.

They made small talk. He congratulated her on the start of the watercolour again. She neither returned to metaphysics nor did she quiz him on what he was doing out on an afternoon as predictably foul as this. It was now a downpour outside.

'How are the children coping?' she asked, as if they were still teenagers.

Duncan shrugged, 'Fine. I mean . . . no obvious problems. None that I can see, anyway.'

'Just as they can't see yours.' She replied with a bourbon cream hovering at her mouth. 'But you know, to my mind, the problems of the young and . . . well, older people, are the one and the same. They're puzzled by the same questions, none really wiser than the other.'

Duncan rose to leave.

'Borrow a book, if you like,' she said as she disappeared again, this time to look for her coat. She insisted on giving him a lift back to the house. He would have normally refused but he couldn't resist her three aids to the Russian language and he did not want them ruined by the rain.

Russian is the official language of Russia; an Indo-European language belonging to the East Slavonic branch. Duncan spent the whole of that evening, after Susan had finally gone, reading the three introductions. *There are thirty-two letters in the Russian alphabet . . . . The Cyrillic script derives from . . .*

It was near midnight before he had grasped the rudimentaries of how to use the dictionaries. He wanted to be systematic even if that meant delaying learning the truth. He had to be sure he could believe what he was about to discover. But he was too tired to trust himself with the task that night and so he went to bed feverish for the morning.

The next day the sun shone so brightly into his room that at first he thought he had forgotten to close the curtains. He shaved and washed as usual but skipped breakfast and went straight to the task. Translating the month didn't matter at the moment. The priority was to decipher what the letters said and to find a clue as to who they could be from. So he started with the word *Dear* to confirm that that was what was written and to revise some of the lessons he had learnt the night before. Sure enough – Дорогой – in ten painful minutes could be converted to *Dear*. He moved on to the next word – *Irene*, he presumed. The letters must start *Dear Irene*. But no, the Russian script didn't match at all. Perhaps it was a Russian name equivalent to Irene in English, he wondered and began the job of transcribing the strange symbols into English letters. It really didn't strike him until he had translated the second-last symbol, but he made himself finish the word before he dropped his pen: DUNKAN, it said.

The two words of Russian that he had translated: *Dear Duncan*.

Another script, another language, even her handwriting looked different; but these were Irene's words. Her two words written for him.

Duncan put on his jacket, stuffed the six letters into a pocket and searched frantically for his car keys. He was halfway down the drive before he remembered the other letter, the one he had found on her grave, and that the Minister might need the help of her books.

He caught her as she was leaving the cottage. He parked behind her car and ran to her.

'Duncan! Are you all right? What's the matter?'

'Read me them!' he said, thrusting the letters to her chest. 'Read me them now. Please.' He tried to dry his eyes but the tears wouldn't stop.

'Come in Duncan. Come inside.' The Minister took him by the arm. He fell into a chair.

'Please,' he pleaded. 'Please read them!'

She stretched the crumpled letters and studied them carefully, rearranging their order. She then muttered to herself in Russian.

'In English. Read me them in English!' Duncan sat forward in the chair.

'This one is the first,' she began, '*11ᵗʰ June 2000. Dear Duncan . . .*' But there she stopped.

'What? What does she say?'

The Minister sat down beside him holding out the pages in front of them.

'Duncan, the rest is personal. She only meant for you to read it.'

'They're in Russian. I can't read Russian.'

'You could learn.'

'Learn? Now? I'll never . . .'

'You can. I take lessons, twice a week.'

He stared at her. 'Did Irene . . . ? Was it here that she . . . ?'

The Minister placed the letters on the table.

'It'll take me forever.'

'You have all the time in the world, Duncan. All the time you need.'

That afternoon, as he began studying at the kitchen table for his first lesson in Russian, Duncan felt it again: he was being watched. But from where? Suddenly, the window started rattling. He looked up. The noise stopped but he saw the striped head of a blue tit staring curiously into the house. The bird jumped up from the ledge where it had been resting and began pecking at the glass again. Eventually it gave up and settled down once more, looking straight at Duncan with a puzzled expression.

Duncan left his books open as he rose and walked to the drawer where the peanuts were kept. For how long had he left the bird feeder empty?

Nodding Off

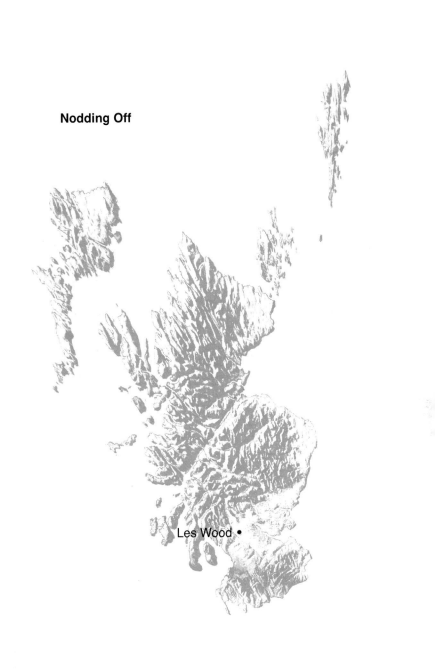

Les Wood •

'Mmmmmnnno eddy et . . .'
'Whit dae ye mean, yer no ready yet? Fur Chrissakes, cumoan we've no goat aw day!'

Kenny and me are gaun up the toon. He wants tae buy the new Rangers away tap, an Ah'm takin him up tae the SportsWorld shoap in Sauchiehall Street. It'll mean the full kit-n-kiboodle though. The chair, the warm claes, the walkin aw the wey in cos we canny get the chair oan the fuckin buses. He'll probably want tae take the dug anaw.

Funny thing wi Kenny, dugs don't seem tae gie a fuck aboot him no bein right. It's aw wan tae thaim. Love me an Ah'll love ye back – that seems tae be their motto. Kenny an Sparky go everywhere thegither.

Ah don't like yasin the word spastic masel. Ah hate the wey folk'll shoarten it tae spazzy or spasmo or somethin. Kenny's goat whit the doacters caw *quadriplegic athetoid cerebral palsy*. Bit ae a moothful, Ah know. Ah usually just explain tae folk he's goat a bad muscle disorder. Except it's no muscles, it's his nerves. Or somethin. Makes him aw scrunch up an gie jerks an twists an things. Wance, he dislocatit his hip wi aw the writhin he wis daein. Pair bugger.

Pair bugger or no, Ah don't know if Ah can be arsed lukin efter him *and* the bloody dug though. It's bad enough huvin tae push that bastartin chair aw ower the place, but tae huv tae watch oot for Sparky anaw . . . it's jist too much. Ah go through tae Kenny's bedroom tae broach the subject. 'Heh, Kenny jist me an you the day, eh pal?'

Too late. Sparky's sittin up on Kenny's knee gettin a wee cuddle. Well, as good a cuddle as Kenny can gie him. Kenny's goat wan erm in his shirt, but the other sleeve's aw twisted an fankled an he's kinda

161

aw caught up in it. The two ae them turn tae luk at me.

'Arrky tae,' Kenny says. 'Wwwwanny ake Parky.'

'Aw, cumoan Kenny,' Ah plead. 'Can we no jist make it the two ae us, jist this wance?' Kenny's face faws. That's no exactly true, Ah suppose. Kenny's face is aye aw gaun. Girnin an twitchin an slaverin. But Ah've known him fur aw his nineteen years an Ah can tell when he's disappintit. The dug disnae help maitters by lettin oot a wee whine.

'Mmmon Immo, Paarrky tae'

'Don't caw me Simmo, it's Simon,' Ah say. Ah hate Simmo. Fuckin ned's name.

'Awwight, Imon. Wwwwanny ake Parrky.'

The dug luks fae him tae me. Fuck's sake. Whit can Ah dae? He's ma wee brother, he's disadvantaged (tae pit it fuckin mildly), he's no goat much gaun fur him in life. Ah make a big show ae lettin oot a big fuckin sigh. 'Right, awright . . . but Ah'm no huvin him oan the leash. Ye can jist tie him oantae yer chair. Awright?'

Kenny smiles his twisted smile. 'Mmma brirr,' he says, an laughs.

Ah help Kenny get dressed, pullin oan his tracksuit gear an tyin his trainers fur him.

'Right, wait here a meenit,' Ah tell him.

'Bubbry hat!' he shouts.

'Whit de ye want tae wear that fur?' Ah start tae argue, but get his Burberry baseball cap oot the drawer aw the same an fling it ower tae him. 'Wait here.'

Ah get his chair fae the loaby an take it doon tae the front ae the close. The chair's heavy. No wan ae they lightweight joabs wi the big wheels fur propellin it alang. Kenny's no goat the co-ordination fur that. Jist four wee wheels at each coarner, a wee table at the front fur Kenny tae pit his things oan an another wee tray unnerneath fur shoppin an that. Ah unfold it an set it at the fit ae the stairs. Ah huv a quick luk roon tae make sure nae bastirt is gonnae lift it while Ah'm away back up the stairs. Aw quiet.

Ah go back up an get Kenny. Ah huv tae cairry him doon aw three flights, an he's heavy tae. Nae wunner ma back's gien me fuckin gyp these days. Every day it's the same: take him oot – the chair, then Kenny; take him in – Kenny, then the chair. Christ almighty, it should be a fuckin Olympic sport. Ah'd win it. By rights we should huv a grun flair flat, bit wur Da's never boathered tryin tae sort it oot wi the cooncil.

Ah get Kenny intae the chair an settled, ask him if he's goat his money an he gies a wee nod. He's been savin fur months fur this bloody jersey, an Ah've telt him he's wastin his dosh oan ower-priced tripe. But it's whit he wants, so who the fuck am Ah tae stoap him? His baseball cap's squinty, so Ah fix it fur him.

We start tae set aff, when Kenny lets oot a yell. 'Nnnndug!'

'Oh aye, Ah nearly forgoat,' Ah lie. 'Hing oan an Ah'll get him.'

Back up the bloody stairs again, an there's Sparky sittin ahin the door, tail waggin.

'Cumoan ya wee bugger.' He jumps tae his feet, or paws Ah suppose, an Ah clip him oantae his leash an it's back doon the stairs. Again.

Ah fasten Sparky oantae the haunle ae Kenny's chair yasin a clove hitch or a granny knot or some such fuckin boy scout type ae thing. At last, we're away.

Except we're no. We don't get a hunner yairds when Ah hear this scrapin noise ahin us. Ah turn roon an there's Sparky tryin tae squat doon an dae a shite, but he's gettin trailed alang by Kenny's chair. It's kinda funny in a wey.

We stoap an wait fur him tae dae his business. When he's feenished, Ah get a wee placcy bag oot ma poakit, fold it ower ma haun an yase it tae pick up the shite fae the pavement. Ah'm no daein this oot ae any civic duty mind ye. It's jist that wance Ah wis takin Kenny back fae somewhere or other an Ah rolled his chair ower a big turd on the street. It wis wan that Ah'd remembered Sparky hud done earlier. Jist like Blue Peter. Fuck's sake, it took me bastirtin ages tae get the keech oot ae the wee grooves oan the wheels. Hud tae yase a knife fae the cutlery drawer tae get it aw oot. So, Ah don't want tae go through aw *that* again, hence the wee bags.

There's nae bin aboot so Ah tie up the jobby bag an pit it oan the wee tray unnerneath Kenny's wheelchair until we come acroas wan.

We set aff again.

It takes us aboot forty-five meenits tae walk aw the wey intae the toon. Glesca's a hilly place an, whit wi the combined weight ae Kenny an his chair, an me pushin it at a fair lick, Ah'm knackered by the time we get tae Sauchiehall Street. We fun the SportsWorld shoap an see that there's a wee ramp fur wheelchairs tae get in. Thing is though, cos Kenny's chair isnae yer standard type ae wheelchair, it's too wide tae fit oan the ramp properly. It keeps tiltin aff tae wan side whenever Ah try tae get it oan, an Ah cannae manage tae push it up tae the door. An anywey, even if Ah goat it tae the door, Ah don't think it wid fit through, it's that wide. Ah huv tae gie up.

Ah pit the brake oan, an park the chair ootside the shoap windae. The dug must be tired tae, since right away he jist curls up at the side ae the chair. Kenny's lukin a wee bit disappintit again. Ah know he'd been lukin furrit tae gaun intae the shoap an huvin a browse an that. But there's nuthin Ah can dae aboot it.

'There's nuthin Ah can dae aboot it,' Ah tell him.

'Ahnnnoo,' he says.

Ah go intae the inside poakit ae his jaicket an fish out five tenners. 'Ye'll no be gettin much chinge oot ae this,' Ah say. 'Ye sure, noo? This is whit ye want tae spen yer money oan?' Ah ask. Kenny nods. 'Righty-hoh then, wan Rangers away tap comin up.' Ah walk up the ramp tae the shoap door. 'Ah'll no be too long, jist wait there tae Ah come oot.' As if he'd suddenly decide he'd want tae take Sparky fur a dauner doon tae Buchanan Galleries while Ah'm in, Ah laugh tae masel.

Inside the shoap they've goat an amazin range ae things – videos, scarves, bomber jaickets, photies an the like. They aw cost a fuckin fortune but. Ah fun the rack wi the away taps an pick oot wan that's the right size fur Kenny. Ah'm feelin a wee bit sorry fur him no bein able tae get intae the shoap an that, so Ah check how much money Ah've goat oan me an decide tae get his name printed oan the back as a wee surprise. Fifty pee a letter. Thank fuck wur name's Barr, an no somethin lik MacWilliams or some other long-named bastirts.

Ah take the jersey ower tae the lassie at the wee coonter where they sort oot the letters an tell her whit Ah want.

'No problem sir,' she says. 'Two minutes and it'll be done.' She takes the shirt through the back somewhere.

She's nice. Talks nice tae. Ca'd me 'Sir'. Ah gie a wee smile tae masel. Lassies hardly ever talk tae me. Maistly cos Ah've always goat Kenny in tow. It gets oan ma wick sometimes. Ah know Ah'm the only wan that can luk efter him – wur Ma's deid an wur Da's an auld alky that disnae gie a fuck aboot either ae us. Especially Kenny. When wur Ma wis alive she aye said that since the day Kenny wis born the wey he wis, wur Da didnae even pick him up. Never cuddled him or anythin. Christ, this is beginnin tae sound like fuckin 'Nobody's Child'. So . . . Ah know there's only me that'll see tae him. But it gets tae me. Ah canny even get a proper joab cos Ah've goat full-time employment lukin efter him. An lassies? Well ye can fuckin forget that! Whit chance wid Ah staun? Ah widnae even know how tae chat them up right. Wi Kenny hingin aboot me lik a fuckin ba an chain, lassies widnae even gie me a second luk. But Ah'm in *here* masel. Naebody knows aboot Kenny in *here*. Mibbe when this lassie comes back wi the shirt Ah'll try an talk tae her, see how Ah get oan. Naw, that wid probably no work. She mair than likely gets chatted up by the customers aw the time, an, anywey, she luks the type that's goat a boyfriend awready.

Jist as Ah'm thinkin aw this she comes back. She shows me the letterin an it luks good. 'That's magic,' Ah say.

'No bother, sir,' she says back.

Ah gie her the money an she pits the shirt an receipt in a bag fur me. She hauns me back ma chinge an Ah've decided, tae Hell wi it,

Ah'm gonnae say somethin tae her. Jist somethin nice an simple.

But jist as Ah'm aboot tae open ma mooth Ah hear a commotion ootside the shoap. There's shoutin an laughin an a dug barkin. *Whit noo?* Ah think

Ah grab ma bag an stuff the chinge intae ma poakit. 'Thanks miss,' Ah say ower ma shooder as Ah run taewards the door. *'Miss'*? Fuck's sake, whit am Ah sayin?

Ah get ootside an see whit's gaun oan. There's a bunch ae guys hingin aboot Kenny's chair, laughin at him. Seven or eight ae them. They're staunin there in their white Kappas an expensive trainers, an their makin fun ae him. Kenny's twitchin an spasmin like crazy. He's moanin – a sickenin low noise, nae words, even by Kenny's standards. It's pure fear. Sparky's barkin an strainin at his leash tryin tae get at them, but they're staunin jist beyond his reach. A man walkin by tells the boays tae lay aff but they tell him tae fuck right off. Kenny's still wailin – he canny see me yet.

Ah hear wan ae them say 'Heh, that's some song yer singin spazz-boy.' He spits on Kenny. It's then that Ah notice that they've aw been daein it. Kenny's covered in spit – big greasers – oan his claes an oan his face. That's when Ah loas it.

'Ya fuckin cunts!' Ah shout, lashin oot wi ma fit tae try an kick the nearest wan. He dodges oot the wey an Ah miss. 'Ya absolute fuckin bastirtin cunts!' Ah fire it oot hard, emphasisin the first letter ae every word. Ah'm nae hard man, faur fae it, but Ah've learned that if ye talk the talk, wanks like these will always assume ye can walk the walk tae. It works. They back aff a bit, still laughin an pointin. A few mair passers-by shake their heids an tell them they'll get the polis tae them. The neds urnae bothered.

Ah bend doon tae talk tae Kenny. He's aw gaun noo, legs an erms dancin aboot, oot ae control, flingin theirsels oot ae the chair. Ah think he's mibbe gonnae hurt hissel. 'Calm doon Kenny, calm doon,' Ah say, tryin tae be reassurin. Ah take ma hanky oot an start tae wipe the spittle aff his face.

'Nnnnnggghhh,' says Kenny. 'Awwwie aaggghh!'

'They're pricks Kenny, jist pricks. Cumoan let me get ye clean.'

The neds see that Ah'm no peyin them any attention an they gie us a final 'Ya coupla fannies!' an start tae move aff doon the street. Folk gie them a wide berth.

Kenny's still aw agitatit. 'Awwwie aaggghh!! Awwwie aaggghh!!'

Ah start tae realise this isnae jist mair moanin or wailin – he's tryin tae say somethin. Ah'm usually dead good at pickin up oan his speech, Ah never really huv a problem unnerstaunin him. But Ah canny quite get this.

'Awwwbie.' He convulses in the chair, throwin wan ae his legs straight oot. But he's makin a real effort tae say whit he wants tae say. Sparky's still a barkin machine at wur side.

'Awwwbie.' He waits. 'Bbbaaaggghh!' Again he stops, draws his braith. He's tryin his best, an Ah concentrate as hard as Ah can. 'Paarrrrkky . . . . Schzawwwbie bbbaaaggghh!!'

Suddenly Ah've goat it! It jist clicks intae place. 'Oh, ya dancer. Fuck me Kenny, that's good!'

Ah hunt unnerneath the wheelchair an, sure enough, there's Sparky's wee jobby bag. Except it's no that wee. Ah'd clean forgoat it wis there. But no Kenny. Ah luk doon the street an judge the distance tae the nearest wan. It's no that faur. Ah feel the weight ae the bag. Kenny's stoaped moanin an he's lukin up at me. 'Dae it,' he says, clear as a bell.

Ah throw the bag in a high arc, takin it ower the crowd taewards the gang ae neds. 'Heh, bawbags!' Ah shout at the tap ae ma voice. They turn tae luk, tae see whit Ah'm shoutin at them fur noo. Jist as they turn, the bag splatters right intae the face ae the biggest wan. It bursts, sprayin shite aw ower two or three ae the ither yins. The big wan hus a luk ae pure horror oan his face an Ah can see even fae here that he's goat some shite in his mooth. He stoops doon and pukes his load in the middle ae the street. The rest ae them are wunnerin whit the fuck's gaun oan.

Ah take the opportunity ae the general confusion tae turn Kenny roon an leg it up the street an oot the road afore they can begin tae think ae comin efter us an gie us a right good kickin. We get tae Hope Street an Ah take wan mair glance ower ma shooder afore turnin the coarner. The bastirts are lukin aboot fur us, bit they cannae see us. The big wan's still heavin his guts up.

Ah slow doon a wee bit an guide Kenny ower tae a shoap doorway. Ah park the chair an kneel doon in front ae him. 'Ye awright, Kenny?' Ah ask. His face twists and flexes an slevers drip oot ae his mooth. Ah get ma hanky, an yase it tae wipe the rest ae the greasers aff him.

'Mmmmmppphhh . . .' he says. 'Ffffkinn cnnntts.' His erm starts contortin, curlin up unner his oxter. 'Cnnntts oook mmmaa at.' It's only noo Ah notice his Burberry baseball cap's away. He loves that stupit hat.

'Ye want tae go back an get it aff them?' Ah ask, hopin he'll say naw.

'Arrssoles cnnnuv it, wwwwiddnae wwwantit bbbaack nnnnooo.' He throws his heid back, bangin it aff the back ae the chair. 'Get mmme a pppint nnnstteed.'

Ah laugh, mair wi relief than anythin else. 'Kenny, ye deserve mair than wan. Sparky's bag, man that wis a cracker!' Kenny starts shakin, an Ah think he's laughin tae, bit when a luk at him closer Ah see he isnae. He's greetin. Tears are runnin' doon his cheeks an he starts rockin back an furrit in his chair. Ah've seen him lik this afore an Ah know no tae say anythin. It's jist pure frustration that he's coat up in a boady that disnae work, an there's nothin he can dae aboot it. An nothin he'll ever be able tae dae aboot it. Pair bastirt's gonnae be lik this fur the duration.

Folk are startin tae stare at us, an Ah think – youse know hee-haw dain't youse? Ye jist take it aw fur grantit that youse can walk aboot, an run, an drive, an play fitba, go tae nightclubs, huv sex, huv weans . . . huv a life. Ye don't know whit it's like tae be loaked intae yer ain boady, never able tae dae anythin normal fur yersel. Huvin tae rely oan other folk tae dae even the simplest things fur ye, lik wipe yer arse or blaw yer nose, or feed ye, or take ye intae toon tae buy a fuckin Rangers jersey. Ah'm startin' tae get angry an Ah realise it's no really aboot thaim at aw. It's aboot me. There's fuck all wrang wi' me, an Ah might as well be a fuckin spastic lik Kenny fur aw the wey ma life's turnin oot. Ah luk at him bobbin aboot in his chair, turned in oan hissel an Ah realise Ah'm nae different. Ma hale life is jist turned in oan itsel.

Ah shut ma eyes an let oot a sigh. 'Right, cumoan then,' Ah say an start tae push the chair up the street, Sparky trottin alang at wur side.

We stoap aff at Barney's, a good wee pub oan the wey hame. The customers are maistly aw auld guys an they know us, an usually don't gie Kenny any grief, jist accept him fur whit he is. Wullie, the barman, keeps a plastic beaker wi a lid behin the bar fur Kenny's pint – it stoaps Kenny fae throwin the lager aw ower hissel when he's tryin tae guide it tae his mooth. Sparky gets a bag ae crisps oan the hoose.

We don't speak much. Ah cannae be boathered, an Kenny's still too worked up tae form his words right. Or mibbe he cannae be boathered either. He jist takes wee sips ae his lager, sookin it oot fae the wee pourer thing oan the tap ae his beaker. He's no really supposed tae take alcohol wi his medication. The doacter says it'll make his spasms worse, but tae be honest it usually calms him right doon. An he likes it tae, so whit the fuck.

Ah show Kenny his Rangers tap wi his name oan it an he brightens up a bit. Gie's me wan ae his crooked smiles. 'Nnnnnaannnkks brirr.' Ah shake ma heid an smile back.

It starts tae get daurk, so Ah decide we'll make tracks afore the street lights come oan. Kenny gies Wullie a shaky wee wave as he hauns his beaker back ower the bar. 'See youse later lads,' Wullie says as we head oot the door.

Efter aboot five meenits a realise Ah'm burstin fur a pish. Ah curse masel fur no gaun back at the pub. Ah'd hud three pints in quick succession, Ah shoulda known Ah'd be needin.

Further up the road Ah can see the turn-aff that leads doon tae the canal towpath. Thank fuck. Ah'll be able tae head doon there an huv a slash if there's naebody aboot.

Ah manage tae steer Kenny's chair doon ontae the gravelly path that runs alangside the canal, an Ah let Sparky aff his leash tae run aboot daft. He's no hud a chance aw day. We move further up the path roon a bend that takes us oot ae sight ae the road. The coast is clear so a slip ma tadger oot and let go a big streamie intae the canal. The watter makes a nice tinklin sound. Ah huv a wee luk aroon as Ah feenish aff. It's kinda peaceful an a big yella moon hings in the sky atween the trees oan the oappposite bank. Ah turn tae see if Kenny sees it, but he's fell asleep. Fur the first time the day he's relaxed, slumped ower in his chair, a wee bit ae drool dribblin oot the coarner ae his mooth.

Ah staun behin his chair an shut ma eyes. Ah breathe deep an snoak in the cool air. It smells good. Ah can hear Sparky snufflin aboot in the bushes. Ah open ma eyes again an luk doon at Kenny's heid lollin tae wan side. Ah think aboot whit his life must be like. Wunner if it really is a life worth livin at aw. An Ah compare it tae mine. Is mine worth livin? Livin like this? Huvin tae luk efter Kenny fur the rest ae ma days. A life withoot dignity? Fur baith ae us? Ah take haud ae Kenny's chair an move it slowly tae the edge ae the path till the front wheels are hingin ower the watter. Ah feel the weight ae the chair, balance it aginst a wee bit ae pressure oan the haunles. Whit wid happen if Ah jist let go, tipped the chair ower the side? Ah widnae be able tae get Kenny back oot that wis for sure. He wid jist slip tae the boattom ae the canal. The watter wid close ower him, an he wid cease tae be. Ah could say it wis an accident.

Kenny's awake an he luks up at me.

'Nnnnnooadafff.'

'Aye, ye did, ye noaded aff there.'

'Nnnaww. Mmmnnnooadaff.'

'Naw, Ah don't suppose ye ur.'

Ah luk up at the moon, an Ah haud ma braith.

Manniit

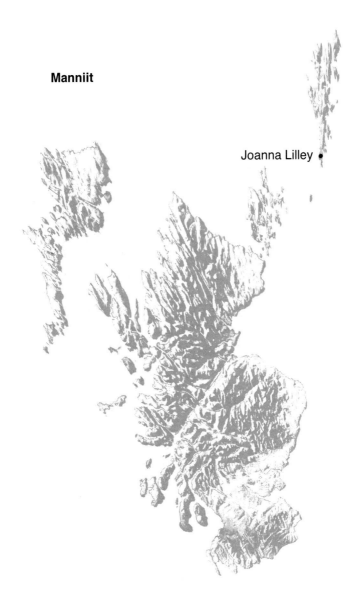

Joanna Lilley •

It's her second day here in this place where water, land and sky merge, but she hasn't met him yet.

She's e-mailed him regularly over the last few months, imagining winged envelopes of electricity flying over the Clyde, across a curved ocean, above the ice floes. Communication is easy, yet she has no idea how the messages pass from one computer to another or why the words and letters don't get jumbled up. She is the subject of a technological oligarchy. Perhaps e-mails transmit only because she believes in them. Faith is the transducer.

In his e-mails, he calls himself Kenu, so Jenny does too.

Really, he has two first names. His mother named him Peter but when he was seventeen he decided that he would be Kenujuak. He knew who he was; evidently his mother, when she first met him, didn't.

But he says – writes – that he understands. He knows how it was then, when there was significance in giving your child a white name. That if thirty thousand people were dissolved into the rest of the world's five or so billion they would be as imperceptible to the taste buds as a teaspoon of sugar in an Olympic-sized swimming pool. And perhaps it was better to get the dissolution over with as quickly as possible.

His mother is different now. She crouches closer to her wide land. Kenu writes to Jenny that he thinks she's becoming an angakok, a shaman, and that her reincarnation has begun too soon, before her body has died. He isn't sure whether a transmigration has already taken place, or if there are two inua, or souls he explains, present. It seems like it; he can see a struggle in the changing rhythm of her muscles. Sometimes, one of her hands is as cold as snow while the other is hotter than the melted wax of the seal-fat candle she lights to read herself to sleep. She marvels at this, reaches out her fingers for her son to feel.

Last night, when Jenny heard Kenu's voice on the telephone for the first time, she was surprised not to recognise it after speaking to him for so many months electronically. She hadn't, she realised, been expecting him to sound so male, or so North American. He even had the rise of intonation at the end of his sentences that she's so familiar with from Australian soap operas but that she knows is native to this continent too, originating, she believes, down in the south, where the states are ostensibly united.

She's due at his studio in less than an hour but she can't leave her building yet because it's minus three degrees outside and if she arrives too early she'll freeze. Each time she's gone outside so far, she's been sliding on the navy salopettes she went skiing in when she was at school. When she first pulled them on over her trousers she was simultaneously surprised that they still fitted and disappointed that they weren't any looser. She's always been big, fleshy as a seal.

It's quite easy to find her way. He's given her good directions to his studio and she's already familiar with some of the streets from yesterday's explorations to the edges of the town to look for the joins between snow, sea and sky. As she walks, she folds her street map around the piece of paper she wrote Kenu's directions on and eases them both, crackling, into her pocket. She doesn't want to look like the tourists she sees from time to time.

The town isn't picturesque; there's an igloo-shaped church which she visited yesterday but little else besides scattered, boxy buildings, mostly white but sometimes pale yellow, blue or red. They all look as if they have been erected where they are because that's where the materials happened to have been set down. Apparently each one is built on stilts dug into frozen earth, although she's seen no evidence of this, perhaps because of the snow. When she rakes the snow she's walking on with the toe of her boot, the earth is loose underneath; none of the roads are paved here.

She passes a school that looks like an enormous plastic toy brick on which a child has painted geometric lines with a hog-hair paintbrush. At the corner of the street where she should find Kenu's studio she smiles at the octagonal red stop sign; it's bilingual and underneath the English word is one she cannot read, pronounce or write.

Arriving at Kenu's studio eighteen minutes early, she turns to walk back to the Northern Store, where an apple costs three dollars, planning to absorb the warmth between the aisles. A voice, almost familiar, calls out to her and she undoes her turn. He has a beautiful face. One she would like to touch with the tips of her fingers and then sculpt, pressing on pellets of soft clay to form those rounded cheekbones, scraping back to create the smiling brow below a short black fringe. But she hasn't played with clay since she was a child.

He can't have been here long as he's still wearing his coat, one of those broad padded jackets that look as if they need to be kept inflated with a bicycle pump. The bottom of it only comes down to his hips, revealing the frailty of his pelvis. His trousers are loose and made out of a silky material that looks too thin to keep him warm in this weather. Perhaps, like her, he wears overtrousers when he's outside or perhaps to him this isn't such a cold day. It's spring, after all.

As he removes his coat she sees there is a bar of strength in his swimmer's shoulders, hooked between his clavicles and his scapulas. She can see now how he, lean as a wolf, can do it. Hammer and chisel rocks and stones. Strap boulders to his snowmobile and bump across the wiry tundra.

'It's weird to meet you at last,' he tells her. She's glad he's said it.

'You're not how I imagined you,' she says, then regrets it, for not only is it a cliché but now he'll ask her what she had imagined. But he doesn't ask and so she wonders why.

She leans against a workbench, squashing her bottom which feels broad in the salopettes, but she's too cold to take them off.

'Would you rather work while we talk,' she says, 'While I ask you questions? Do you mind if I watch you work? Is it okay if I tape our conversation?'

'Yes to everything,' he says. 'On one condition?'

'What?'

'That you'll have dinner with me tonight? With me and my mom at home?'

Jenny smiles. 'That's difficult,' she says. 'I'm vegetarian.'

Kenu laughs loudly. 'You never told me that in your e-mails. You sure are in the wrong place, you know?' He laughs again.

Jenny knows. Her fellow students at the university have spent the last year reminding her.

'Come anyway,' says Kenu. 'No problem. Hey, you should take those off, you know.' He's nodding at her legs, sounding parental. 'Or you'll be cold when you go back out.' He pronounces 'out' as if it rhymes with 'boat'. She repeats it inside her head, trying to remember it. Hoping he'll say it again when she's got the tape running, not that it has anything to do with her research.

'I'm already cold,' she says.

'There's a stove over here,' he tells her, beckoning, and as she notices the black pipe rising up through the low ceiling she smells the warmth. Beyond it, there's a collection of unsculpted stone, ordered by material and size. Some cut into blocks, others looking as if only the weather has ever touched them. Serpentine, soapstone, marble, argillite, quartzite, bone, antler, ivory. Jenny opens her rucksack and takes out the tape recorder, and her notebook and pen too, hoping the ink isn't congealed from being outside. She has a list of questions on a sheet of paper slotted into a plastic see-through file.

After she's interviewed him and Kenu has gone home for lunch, Jenny rushes back through the town to her room to write up her notes. The rushing makes her sweat and for a time she sits at her desk, shivering as her body cools down more quickly than a shallow bath. In under five hours, she'll go back to the studio to take up her dinner invitation. It will be dark then; she's glad she already knows the way.

On her return trip, she discovers there's an optimum pace at which to move. If she walks too slowly, her toes and fingers grow numb then start to ache, while if she walks too quickly she sweats and that makes her cold as soon as she stops. She looks around for other people, hard to see at first in the dull street lighting, then imitates the pace at which they are walking.

At the studio, she knocks quietly and enters wordlessly. Kenu is working on a different piece. The abstracted bear-man of the morning has been put away, or pushed away, supposes Jenny, as it must be heavy. Kenu raises one hand to acknowledge her arrival and she sits, trying to make her body look relaxed, to denote that she's happy to wait. She watches him for many minutes until he straightens up, pushes his forefingers into the base of his spine, and gently returns a mallet and a toothed chisel to the correct empty spaces on the workbench. Then he hefts the lump of serpentine from the sandbag it has been resting on, places it on a sturdy shelf and drapes a cloth over it.

'I don't want its spirit to escape while I've gone,' he jokes. 'I'm having trouble finding it as it is and I need it to stay inside until I've finished.'

From what Jenny had seen, there's a bird spirit residing in the stone, one green wing unfolding. It reminds her of the arctic skuas she has read about. They have a cuckoo mind. Rather than fish for themselves and even though they can, they chase other birds, forcing them to drop or disgorge their catch mid-air, seizing it before it hits the water.

'Your mum's remembered I'm vegetarian?' asks Jenny as they walk to Kenu's house. She is trying to concentrate on the route they take so that she can find her way back. 'I really don't want to be a nuisance.'

177

'Sure she's remembered. She doesn't quite understand how you can survive without meat,' he laughs, 'or why on earth you should want to, but . . .' Kenu pauses, changes tone, 'you see, traditionally, if you didn't eat meat you'd never have survived here. We have only really two months when you can eat plants and berries.'

'Thank God for the white invasion of the north,' says Jenny, wryly. 'Bringing its three-dollar apples and its peanut butter and jelly.'

'And white sliced bread,' adds Kenu. 'What's the point of PB and J without white sliced bread to roll it up in?'

They are silent for a few moments and Jenny wonders if all those e-mails were a bad idea. They should have saved up some words to say to each other with their voice boxes rather than their mailboxes.

'Hey, Jenny,' says Kenu softly. 'Have you ever tried sculpting serpentine? You'd love it, I bet, it's so smooth. Forgiving. Soft as skin sometimes. And don't tell me academics never have a go at these things. I saw the way you were looking at my supplies, my gatherings.'

'Yeah, well,' admits Jenny. 'I did a bit when I was a child. Clay mostly, though I liked the idea of woodcarving.'

'I like woodcarving,' says Kenu. 'I'm never sure whether to get into it or not. I mean, wood is scarce round here traditionally. But then I use non-native stone, so why don't I carve wood too?' Jenny can tell he's not intending to bring the conversation back to him. He's lending her one of his doubts as if to encourage her to lend him one of hers in return.

Jenny laughs and Kenu looks at her. 'I was a bit of a disaster with woodcarving,' she says. 'When I was a child, about ten I think, I'd seen some photographs of some wooden sculptures in one of my mum's magazines. These sculptures were abstract, very intricate, but not fussy. Anyway, I went up to my bedroom that night and suddenly started noticing how much wood there was in my room, bed, bookshelves, window frames, chair, desk, and how plain it all was. So I got out my penknife – I was a bit of a tomboy – turned my chair upside-down and sat on the edge of my bed. I started carving. Whittling

178

away at this chair leg, making what I thought was a pretty pattern.'

She stops. Kenu is laughing. 'That's great,' he grins, 'that's great.'

'Yeah, especially when my mum was tidying my room a couple of days later and noticed that my chair was wobbly. I'd made that leg shorter than all the others. My parents were furious. They confiscated my penknife and I had to stuff a piece of folded-up paper under the chair leg until I could persuade my dad to saw an inch off the other three legs to even things out. Never did get that penknife back. That was the end of my sculpting career I reckon.'

Kenu chuckles. 'Sounds like just the beginning to me.'

She must have been looking out for them. The front door opens before Kenu has time to take his hand out of his pocket.

'Hello Manniit,' she says, smiling at Jenny. Her small eyes are darker than her son's.

'Mom,' says Kenu, shaking his head and turning towards Jenny. 'Manniit means egg,' he explains. 'It's also what we call the month of June because that's when people go out gathering eggs from the geese and ducks who migrate here. I guess it's the vegetarian month.'

Jenny, giving Kenu her coat to hang up by the door, says, 'June is a woman's name anyway, though I don't think egg is. Why is it you can name someone May, June or April but not January or February?' She's talking too much. Kenu is trying to introduce her to his mother.

'This is my mom, Ovilu,' he says. Jenny holds out her hand and they clutch each other's fingers briefly. 'So, Mom, what's for dinner?'

'We're all vegetarian tonight. Char for everyone.'

Jenny closes her eyes quickly, then, opening them, tries to make them look kind. 'I'm so sorry,' she says. 'I don't eat fish.'

Ovilu looks bewildered. 'Fish isn't meat,' she says.

'I'm so sorry.'

'You don't eat fish?' Kenu looks at her.

'I'm afraid not.' They're both staring at her. 'To eat a fish, you have to kill it. And I couldn't, can't kill anything, so I don't ask that

179

anyone else does it for me. Does that make sense? I really am sorry. I can just eat some bread or something. Peanut butter and jelly,' she smiles at Kenu. 'I'll be fine.'

They leave Jenny standing in the front room and go through to the kitchen together, speaking quietly in Inuktitut. Jenny thinks of leaving the house while they are out of the room. She thinks of offering to go when they come back in. Then, remembering at last her research, she looks around for a way to show that she's making herself at home. She has read that this is how to honour them in their own tradition. Easy to read about. Harder when you're standing in someone's front room, which doesn't truthfully look any different from any others in North America. She gets up and goes to a small bookcase, tilts her head to read the titles. There's a row of crime novels, well-read paperbacks with disintegrating spines. Patricia Cornwell, Minette Walters. A couple of Agatha Christies. Jenny slides *From Potter's Field* from the shelf, sits on the settee and tries to start reading.

As soon as she hears them coming back into the room she snaps the book shut and stands up. Ovilu, face as fixed as a photograph, is carrying a wide-bottomed shallow dish and Kenu brings in a tray with slices of white bread in a basket, a block of cheese, butter and two large jars of peanut butter and blueberry jam. Ovilu nods at Jenny to sit at the table and when Jenny does she realises she's still got the novel in her hand. She places it in the small space between her buttocks and the back of the chair.

'We don't eat as much meat as we used to, or fish,' Ovilu says, sitting down gently, her face relaxing. 'This is arctic char,' she says, indicating the dish with her fingers. 'My old friends sometimes bring me country food but their sons don't hunt so much now. Too busy with government programmes.'

'Country food is what we call, um, hunted food. Our native food?' says Kenu.

'Yes, so I've heard,' says Jenny. Better to say heard than read. 'And typical country food would be caribou? Seal?' she asks, deciding to learn what she thinks she already knows.

'Yes,' says Ovilu, with her first smile since she had called Jenny Manniit.

The book behind Jenny on the chair slips off and slaps the floor. 'Sorry,' whispers Jenny and twists round and down to pick it up. She changes her mind and slides it between the chair legs instead.

'Mom is a great cook,' says Kenu, giving Jenny a grin as she sits upright, face flushed.

'Not a great cook. A listening cook. I paid attention to my elders, remembered what they taught me. But the word 'cook' is not the right word,' says Ovilu with a glance at Kenu who sighs.

'You mean, you don't traditionally cook your food?' says Jenny.

'That's right,' says Ovilu. 'It's sad. You will never taste aalu.'

'Ah-loo?' Jenny tries to repeat.

'I don't think you want to know,' says Kenu.

'Aalu. Delicious. Caribou or seal, though best with seal. Seal is always best. Whatever, the meat must be clean and lean. Cut it up into tiny pieces then add just a few drops of melted fat, then a few drops of blood. Then add uruniq.'

'You really don't want to know,' Kenu is laughing.

Jenny looks at Ovilu.

'The intestine of ptarmigan,' she explains, obsidian-eyed. 'Use your fingers to stir it all up until it's fluffy. Delicious. Very popular.'

There's a warm gleam in Ovilu's eyes now, like an ooze of fresh blood. 'We never imprison animals like your people do. We are never cruel.'

'No,' says Jenny. She looks down and starts to spread peanut butter on a slice of bread.

'So,' says Ovilu, after a few quiet mouthfuls of char. 'You're studying my son?'

'Yes, and other artists. Sculptors.'

'That's why you're here?'

'Yes.'

'Even though you are vegetarian, it's okay for people to carve bone, ivory, antler?'

'I'm mostly interested in stone but, yes, I study other materials too. I have to be thorough.'

'Isn't that hypocritical?'

'Mom,' warns Kenu.

'Yes,' says Jenny. 'It is hypocritical.' She won't win an argument with this woman but she can at least be honest. 'But I have to be vegetarian, it's my way, and I want to study your art, your carving. I don't know why, I just do.'

Ovilu looks at Jenny. 'Okay,' she says.

'I don't have any answers,' says Jenny.

Ovilu takes another quick mouthful of char. 'You are paid? Paid to be here?'

'Kind of. A research grant. It's not much, I have to work too when I'm home.'

Ovilu laughs. 'It's funny. You're paid to study our art.'

Jenny says nothing.

'And yet, there's so little of it.'

Jenny waits.

'There's so little genuine Inuit art in your Western sense, isn't there?' Ovilu waves her hand in the air as if to magic up some more.

'Mom, we've had this conversation a hundred times,' interrupts Kenu. 'Anyway, Jenny has studied other art too, First Nation, and she's interested in our whole culture, how our arts developed. Where it came from. Why things are as they are now.'

Yes, thinks Jenny. He explains it well enough.

'Our so-called art came from necessity,' Ovilu says, talking with her mouth full. 'It had a purpose. Not like those artist communities. They just create prettinesses to sell to the visitors. They don't even use traditional ways.'

Jenny knows she's going to have to say something.

'Tell me, Manniit,' Ovilu continues, after she's swallowed. 'What

182

use are my son's sculptures? Pretty enough. Heavy enough, some of them, but too big for paperweights.'

'Art doesn't have to have a function in the conventional sense,' says Jenny, looking at the bread on her plate. 'Expressing creativity is a function in itself. People still have an urge to create, even when their basic needs are met, especially when their basic needs are met. It's not just about tools and clothes. Sculpture, print-making, sewing. It gives people an outlet, talented people. And you might not know or care, but your son is brilliant.' Jenny pauses, glances at Ovilu but her face is placid. 'Why did you have a son? You didn't need a child to support you, the government is now there to do that. Having a family is a form of creativity too.'

Ovilu smiles at Kenu. 'You know, she's better at this than you are, but then she ought to be. She's gets paid to watch it being done while you get paid to actually do it.'

Kenu walks home with Jenny even though she's tried to persuade him not to; she doesn't want him to apologise for his mother, as she knows he will, because his mother is right. Jenny is worse, perhaps, than the first white men to come here. They at least traded goods, things that were wanted: steel needles, copper kettles and iron-bladed knives in exchange for sealskin clothes and delicate bone carvings. And other things too, it's true. Tobacco and alcohol, things they probably could have done without.

Yet she trades nothing, only takes.

Takes notes and photographs, kidnaps ideas and gives birth to stillborn inspiration. Won't even eat their food.

When Kenu has left her at the door to her building, Jenny goes quietly to her room. Inside, without removing her outdoor clothes, she feels in her pocket and takes out her penknife. She reaches down for the wooden chair at her desk and twists it upside down with one hand. Then she sits down on the bed, wedges a chair leg between her knees and digs her knife into the varnished wood.

The Contributors

S. Akhtar started writing poetry from an early age (but now also writes in prose), has had poems published in Nomad – one poem has also been recorded for Spoken Word – and coordinates Pollokshields Writers' Collective.

Maggie Anderson was born in Rutherglen in 1931. Glasgow Uni was a lot of fun but it made her into an agricultural entomologist of no particular use to anyone, so in 1954 she went to Yemen where she enjoyed a social married life with dental surgeon husband and two daughters. She taught in the Technical Institute of Aden, was a marine biologist for the UN and read the TV news for South Arabian Broadcasting. She packed in a lot of Middle East travel too. During 1972, Jordanhill College polished up her evil eye and she became a happy Glasgow schoolteacher for thirty years. Widowed and retired, she lives in a Pollokshields villa which she lets someone else keep clean while she reads, writes, attends creative writing classes, gardens, socialises and travels – all activities constantly interrupted by a multitude of family, friends and postgrad lodgers.

Elaine Dickie lives in Glasgow and has attended a number of writing classes in the city over the past few years. She has really enjoyed sharing with and learning from other writers and finds the discipline of assignments helps her to focus and produce work that she would otherwise never get around to doing! 'Fins' is her first published story and has given her real motivation to produce more.

Thomas Duncan has been writing for around two years. Initially, he enjoyed writing creative non-fiction with a humourous slant. Over the past year, however, he has witnessed his mother succumb to Alzheimer's disease. He wrote 'Happy Hour' simply as a means of therapy. Ever since, he has kept a detailed journal, not only of his mother's journey into dementia, but of his father's inability to come to terms with her decline. An extract, 'The Lost Art of Communication', recently appeared in a London publication, *The Journal of Dementia Care*. Despite the seriousness of the topic, Thomas has found humour is present in the most unlikely of places. He hopes that the journal will eventually take the form of a book and may even be published. Due to the sensitive nature of the subject matter, the name 'Thomas Duncan' is a pseudonym.

Kirsten Gow was born in Banbury, Oxfordshire, and now lives in Glasgow, but likes to confuse people by telling them that 'home' is a remote island off the west coast of Scotland. Having graduated from university in 1999 with little idea of what she was *supposed* to do next, Kirsten ignored the advice of all of her London-bound friends and moved to Glasgow (with no money, no job and no permanent place to stay!). Since moving to Glasgow she has proactively sought the company of other writers through a series of writing groups and hit a turning point when she joined the Inspiration and Realism class at Strathclyde University. Kirsten has been writing poetry from a young age but more recently has been working on a number of short stories and prose poems and is developing ideas for her first novel.

John Heraghty lives and works in Glasgow. He has been writing for a year. 'When Stevie was Married' is his first story to be published.

Joanna Lilley moved to Scotland nearly six years ago because England was too crowded. She lives in Torphichen and works for a government agency in Edinburgh where she edits a quarterly magazine and does other communications work. A graduate of the M.Litt. in creative writing at the universities of Glasgow and Strathclyde, Joanna is working on her second novel.

David Pettigrew was born in Kilmarnock, lives in Glasgow, and earns his living by editing local history books. He has previously had stories published in the anthologies *Glasgow Kiss* and *Shorts 5* (the Macallan/*Scotland on Sunday* collection, 2002) and at www.orangelabyrinth.com. He is soon to become a student on Glasgow University's M.Phil. course in creative writing.

Saket Priyadarshi is an Indian-born, Glasgow-based government employee who started writing on return from world travels four years ago. Initial ventures were in freelance journalism (travel, feature, music review) for Scottish broadsheets (the *Herald*, *Sunday Herald* and *Scotsman*). His first published fiction was a short story called 'Alice' in *Glasgow Kiss*. Another short, 'Mrs Heggarty', was broadcast as part of a week of 'Scottish Shorts' by Radio 4. 'Translating Duncan' was inspired by a year of solitude and spectacular sunsets in Kintyre. Further projects, including completing a novel and writing more short stories, are worked on in bouts, like the DIY, between the demands and challenges of recent fatherhood.

Sheila Puri has had several stories published in a range of literary anthologies and was a runner up with her collection of eight short stories for a competition run by the Scottish Booksellers Association. This year she was awarded a £5,000 bursary by the Scottish Arts Council to help her work on the novel and short story collection which she is currently trying to write in between looking after her two children, Jaspal and Priya, one already a teenager and another fast becoming one. She lives in Glasgow with her partner Satpal and works part-time for the Health Promotion Department.

Sarah Rauchas grew up in South Africa, came to Scotland thirteen years ago, and now divides her year, unevenly, between the two countries – in a quest to have summer forever, in places of great beauty. While living in Edinburgh and Glasgow, she has danced, choreographed, studied and worked as a researcher. In South Africa she teaches computer science. She spends a lot of time in aeroplanes.

Cynthia Rogerson is from San Francisco and has lived in the Highlands for more than twenty years. Her first novel, *Upstairs in the Tent*, was published in 2002. She has four children and one husband, so far. She teaches creative writing in schools and to adults and is editor for a literary consultancy. She is part-time director at Moniack Mhor Writers Centre.

Sue Rullière was born in Edinburgh, taught for several years in Cambridge and now lives by the sea in East Lothian. Her stories have been published in *Nerve*, *The Eildon Tree* and *Shorts 4* (the Macallan/ *Scotland on Sunday* collection, 2001). She is currently working on a novel.

Laura Stewart has been writing for as long as she can remember and as a child can recall penning some dubious plays and short stories involving kitchen appliances! A couple of years ago she started the Inspiration and Realism creative writing course at Strathclyde University and since then has written a few short stories and has just completed her first novel. She's lived in Glasgow all her life, is married to Pete and has three cats. When not busy writing she enjoys good wine and bad reality television.

Valerie Thornton writes poems and short stories. She has received a Scottish Arts Council writer's bursary, been shortlisted for the Macallan/*Scotland on Sunday* short story prize and her creative writing textbook, *Working Words* (Hodder Educational, 1995), won joint first prize as Times Educational Supplement Scotland and Saltire Society Scottish Educational Book of the Year. Her first collection of poems, *Catacoustics*, was published in 2000 by Mariscat Press. She also has nearly twenty years experience as a creative writing tutor, leading workshops for many different organisations. Some are mainstream groups in colleges and universities, others are more specialized: for blind writers, women-only groups, children, or in addiction or disability resource centres. Before this, she taught English for five years. She was Royal Literary Fund Writing Fellow at Glasgow University, 2001–2003, and is now an RLF Project Fellow, helping teachers in training and in service to develop both their own and their pupils' creative writing skills.

Kate Tregaskis is currently completing her first novel. Prior to committing herself to writing fiction, she worked in the visual arts (as the director of a gallery in Edinburgh) and then subsequently for a short period as a freelance journalist and the co-editor of a visual arts magazine. In 2001 she took part in Critical Voices, a project involving fifty writers, initiated by the Arts Council for the Republic of Ireland. In 2002 she won a New Writers Bursary from the Scottish Arts Council and she was shortlisted this year for the regional final of the Real Writers Short Story Awards. Kate lives and works in Edinburgh.

Les Wood lives in Paisley with Marie, his better half, and Ghillie the dog. He lectures at Glasgow Caledonian University and uses what spare time he has writing short stories and trying to finish a novel. He was a winner of the 2002 Canongate Prize for New Writing.

The final contributions to this book were chosen by:

Meaghan Delahunt, who was born in Melbourne and lives in Edinburgh. In 1997 she won the HQ/Flamingo National Short Story competition in Australia. Her first novel, *In the Blue House*, was longlisted for the 2001 Orange Prize and won the 2001 Commonwealth Writers' Prize for First Novel (Pacific & Asia), the Saltire First Book Award and a Scottish Arts Council Book of the Year award. It has been translated into several languages. She is working on her second novel, *The Prayer Wheel*.

Elizabeth Reeder, who was shortlisted for the Macallan/*Scotland on Sunday* short story competition, and has had numerous stories published in anthologies. She received a Scottish Arts Council bursary to help in the completion of her first novel *Standing Still, Running* and is working on her second novel, *The Fremont Inheritance*. She teaches creative writing in various places, is the Glasgow City Council/Scottish Arts Council Writing Fellow for the North-East of Glasgow and one of the founding board members of OpenInk.

Suhayl Saadi, a widely published short story writer and novelist. In 1997 he won third prize in the Bridport Competition and, in 1999, second prize in the Macallan/*Scotland on Sunday* competition. He also edited the Macallan/*Scotland on Sunday* collection, *Shorts 5*, in 2002. He has worked on many community projects and in 1999 was the recipient of a Millennium Commission Award to set up and run a writers' group aimed at minority ethnic groups in Glasgow. He has worked on the Literature Committee of the Scottish Arts Council and has appeared in New York City and Brussels, and frequently on BBC radio. He is also due to appear at the Edinburgh International Book Festival, 2003. A radio play will be broadcast on BBC Radio Four in 2004. His short story collection, *The Burning Mirror*, was shortlisted for the Saltire First Book Prize, and a novel, *Psychoraag*, will be published in January 2004 by Black and White Publishing. Suhayl lives in Glasgow with his wife and daughter. www.suhaylsaadi.com

Acknowledgements

OpenInk would like to thank everyone who has made this book possible, including:

Our Key Sponsors:
The University of Strathclyde Centre for Lifelong Learning
Glasgow City Council
The Scottish Arts Council

Our Creative Partners:
Café Source at St Andrews in the Square
(0141 548 6020, www.cafesource.co.uk)
Calligraphic Art Services
(01236 423735, http://business.virgin.net/d.tolmie/index)
Gilmorehill G12
(0141 330 5522, www.gilmorehillg12.co.uk)
Jamie Maitland Photography
(07762 827 666, www.ginjaroom.co.uk)

The Founder Sponsors of OpenInk who have provided financial support for our ongoing work:
Angela Baker, Alec Byrne, Laura, Paul, Katie and Jack Ciccantell, Lisa and Paul Climie, Chik Collins, Sandra Davies, Roanne Dods, Lynn Drennan, Peter Falconer, Cathy Fallon, Sheena Gow, Janet Grehan, Amar and Shabana Hussain, Shabana Hussain, David Hutchison, Iris

Kirkpatrick, Rhona Marcuccilli, David and Nancy McAslan, Caroline McAulay, James McDowall, Elaine McFarland, Ailsa McKay, Bruce McKinnon, Frances Monaghan, Kate Mulvey, Sheila Murray, Aidan O'Donnell, Catriona and Neal Padmanabhan, Saied Pourghazi, Frank and Karen Reeder, Debbie Sawatzky, Radha and Smriti Sinha, Peter Stewart, Cyrus Tata, Jean B. Thomson, Fiona and Steve Walton, Rhona Watson, Alec Wersun, and Andrea Williamson.

Other people we couldn't have done it without:
Alec Byrne, Stuart Campbell, Elaine Dickie, Colin Farrell, Lesley Hart, Hamish MacDonald, Catherine McInerney, Carlos Peralta, Sheila Puri, Rik Rogers, Richard Stenlake, Minnie Stevenson, John Stewart, Alix White, Lorna, Frances and Diane at Wise Women, and Elaine at WordPower (www.word-power.co.uk).

All of the friends and family who have supported us during this project.

Everyone who continues to inspire our writing on a daily basis.

About OpenInk

OpenInk is an organisation built on the extensive talent of Scotland's creative community. We believe in creating a unique platform for new Scottish writing and aim to continue to offer writers a chance to shine through our publications and events, and in turn offer readers fantastic and compelling reads.

If you like what we do and would like to find out how you can support OpenInk's work as a sponsor, a creative partner, or in any other way, take a look at our website at:

www.openink.co.uk

or contact us at:

mail@openink.co.uk.